"You don't [barcode] *I ever saw,"*

Luke proclaimed.

Once again, his gaze skimmed over her, this time slower, this time making Sydney's blood simmer and her skin tighten. She crossed her arms over her chest. "Looks can be deceiving. You don't look like a chef, either."

"What'd you expect? The Pillsbury Doughboy™?"

No, she thought. But she would have felt a whole lot safer and infinitely more relaxed if he were.

If she thought he'd looked sexy before, she'd been completely wrong. When this man smiled, a ray of sunshine transformed his face, made his dark eyes burn like coal with a warmth that penetrated the shell she'd built around her heart.

Interrupting her reverie, a plaintive wail started somewhere behind him. A baby's cry.

The most irresistible man she'd met in years… had a baby.

Dear Reader,

The wonder of a Silhouette Romance is that it can touch *every* woman's heart. Check out this month's offerings—and prepare to be swept away!

A woman wild about kids winds up tutoring a single dad in the art of parenthood in *Babies, Rattles and Cribs... Oh, My!* It's this month's BUNDLES OF JOY title from Leanna Wilson. When a Cinderella-esque waitress—complete with wicked stepfamily!— finds herself in danger, she hires a bodyguard whose idea of protection means making her his *Glass Slipper Bride,* another unforgettable tale from Arlene James. Pair one highly independent woman and one overly protective lawman and what do you have? The prelude to *The Marriage Beat,* Doreen Roberts's sparkling new Romance with a HE'S MY HERO cop.

WRANGLERS & LACE is a theme-based promotion highlighting classic Western stories. July's offering, Cathleen Galitz's *Wyoming Born & Bred,* features an ex-rodeo champion bent on reclaiming his family's homestead who instead discovers that home is with the stubborn new owner...and her three charming children! A long-lost twin, a runaway bride...and *A Gift for the Groom*—don't miss this conclusion to Sally Carleen's delightful duo ON THE WAY TO A WEDDING.... And a man-shy single mom takes a chance and follows *The Way to a Cowboy's Heart* in this emotional heart-tugger from rising star Teresa Southwick.

Enjoy this month's selections, and make sure to drop me a line about *why* you keep coming back to Romance. We want to fulfill *your* dreams!

Happy reading,

Mary-Theresa Hussey

Mary-Theresa Hussey
Senior Editor, Silhouette Romance
300 East 42nd Street, 6th Floor
New York, NY 10017

Please address questions and book requests to:
Silhouette Reader Service
U.S.: 3010 Walden Ave., P.O. Box 1325, Buffalo, NY 14269
Canadian: P.O. Box 609, Fort Erie, Ont. L2A 5X3

BABIES, RATTLES AND CRIBS... OH, MY!

Leanna Wilson

Silhouette

ROMANCE™

Published by Silhouette Books

America's Publisher of Contemporary Romance

To my ever faithful, totally honest,
and always supportive critique group:
Tammy Hilz
Betty Seaman
What would I do without y'all?
Thanks Carolyn Wilson for your help and expertise!

SILHOUETTE BOOKS

ISBN 0-373-19378-5

BABIES, RATTLES AND CRIBS... OH, MY!

Copyright © 1999 by Leanna Ellis

This edition published by arrangement with Harlequin Books S.A.

Visit us at www.romance.net

Printed in U.S.A.

Books by Leanna Wilson

Silhouette Romance

Strong, Silent Cowboy #1179
Christmas in July #1197
Lone Star Rancher #1231
His Tomboy Bride #1305
Are You My Daddy? #1331
Babies, Rattles and Cribs... Oh, My! #1378

LEANNA WILSON,

a native Texan, was born and bred in Big D, but she's a country girl at heart. More at home dreaming up stories than lesson plans, she gave up teaching to pursue writing. Once she began putting her stories on paper, it didn't take her long to publish her first Silhouette Romance novel, *Strong, Silent Cowboy*, which won the Romance Writers of America's Golden Heart Award. She's married to a strong, not-so-silent city slicker and lives outside of Dallas with her husband and new baby boy. Even though she's busy singing lullabies and reading to her infant son, she's busy working on her next Romance and enjoys hearing from her readers. You can write to her c/o: Leanna Wilson, P.O. Box 294277, Lewisville, TX 75029-4277.

Dear Reader,

Babies. It's my favorite topic these days. Everywhere I go, I see crying, smiling, cooing, grabbing, toddling, wobbling babies. I think something's in the water. It's definitely catching. Not too long ago I caught baby fever myself. Now I have my very own sweet and cuddly bundle of joy.

Aren't babies wonderful? They're soft and sweet, with that tender skin and rolls of fat. Their smiles not only make their eyes sparkle but put a glow in an adult's heart. It's easy to understand why my hero, Luke, is enamored with his daughter. But, like any new father, he's overwhelmed by the responsibility of changing diapers, waking up for late-night feedings and planning for college tuition. First things first, my heroine, Sydney, tells him. His sweet bundle of joy quickly becomes a parcel of worry. He needs help, and fast! Can Sydney put her own pain aside in order to help out this overwhelmed daddy?

I hope you enjoy Luke and Sydney's story as much as I'm enjoying motherhood.

Happy Reading,

LeAnne Wilson

Chapter One

Babies and rattles and cribs...

Oh, my! Sydney Reede pinched the bridge of her nose as an excruciating headache took hold. She could have kicked herself for getting in this predicament. What the heck was *she* doing planning a baby shower? With frilly pink-and-blue invitations, a list of pin-the-diaper-on-the-baby games and a stack of recipes for succulent hors d'oeuvres, the party should have been as easy as slicing into a chocolate torte. Instead, it was carving a piece out of her heart.

It was Roxie's fault, Sydney thought as she climbed out of her sensible Ford sedan. If Roxie hadn't gotten pregnant...If Roxie hadn't been so nice to Sydney when she'd first moved to Dallas, then Sydney wouldn't feel obligated to give her friend a baby shower. If Roxie wasn't leaving her job vacant after she had her baby, then Sydney wouldn't be trying for the next step up the corporate ladder to fill her friend's position. And she wouldn't be going to a strange man's house for cooking lessons!

Had she lost her ever-lovin' mind?

She remembered her boss saying, "I just love baklava. Consider having it at Roxie's shower. It's such a wonderful dessert with so much family tradition." Ellen had gotten a soft, faraway look in her usually steely eyes. "My mother used to make it for special occasions. What's more special than a baby shower? What was the spice she always added...cinnamon, honey...? I wish I could remember. Oh, you'll figure it out. It really sets it apart from all the other plain baklava."

Plain baklava? The dessert was rich enough to reside in a palace. Sydney had followed the recipe she'd found at the library to the ounce, tablespoon and cup. She'd only added an extra pinch of cinnamon in hopes she'd please her boss's palate and gain favor when she promoted someone, hopefully Sydney, into Roxie's position as account manager.

Her boss wasn't the only one who'd made special requests. Roxie, the mother-to-be, had put in a bid for chocolate soufflé. The vice president of the company had "suggested" crème brûlé. Whatever the heck that was! It sounded difficult, even though the V.P. had sworn it was well worth any extra effort. Well, the worth of it better be a promotion, Sydney thought, figuring she could work out the kinks before the shower as easily as she'd once made animal-shaped pancakes on Saturday mornings for her siblings. Of course, she knew making her boss's and the V.P.'s favorites wouldn't get her Roxie's position. But it couldn't hurt. She wanted to show she was always more than willing, more than capable of going the extra mile...or as in this case...an extra strip of phyllo dough.

But her confidence had fallen as flat as a bad soufflé when she'd pulled her first batch of the baklava concoction from the oven. She'd hoped the pastry would congeal...or puff up...or hold together. It hadn't. It had looked like a volcanic eruption, hardened like a rock and tasted worse than ash.

After wasting an entire weekend trying recipe after recipe, scalding some batches, botching others, Sydney had thrown in her flour-covered apron and reached for the phone. Roxie had started this, and the mother-to-be could bail her out. Or had she only tossed her into the fire?

The broiling Texas heat made the hair at Sydney's nape curl, and she tugged at the short locks she'd had sheared not too long after her divorce last year. Slamming the passenger door closed, she hefted a bag of books over her shoulder and headed for the red-brick house on the corner. The heat seemed to stifle all the noise in the tree-lined neighborhood where the tall oaks formed a canopy over the street. She wondered what kind of a man lived in this quaint area. She knew nothing about Luke Crandall, except what Roxie had told her. He'd won several awards with his culinary skills, and he owned a restaurant in Dallas. Only out of desperation had she agreed to meet him. She still remembered the tingle his deep, rusty voice had caused along her skin when they'd set the date...er...*time* for her cooking lesson.

When she reached the door, she set the heavy bag at her feet, lifted her shoulders and drew in a deep breath to calm her nerves. Searching for the doorbell, she hoped Luke Crandall would answer her prayers.

Before she could press the lighted button, the door swung open with a whoosh. Startled, Sydney gasped and stepped back. The man standing in the doorway literally stole her breath.

"Don't ring the bell." His voice sounded low, urgent, almost desperate. His dark, snapping eyes looked crazed. Sydney's heart skittered to a halt.

This couldn't be the man Roxie had sent her to meet.

This man seemed capable of almost anything, including murder—but not dishing up some delicate canapé. His hands were too big, too rough, like he'd wield an ax instead of a spatula. He could probably snap her in two with a flick of his wrist. And she doubted he'd have any compunction about it.

Her heart jerked back into gear, pumping frantically. Of course, she had the wrong house! Immediately, her gaze shifted above his head to the door frame and checked the numbers against her excellent memory. Had Roxie given her the wrong address?

"Mr. Crandall?" she asked, blinking up at the hawklike intensity of his deep-set, sin-shaded, bloodshot eyes that singed her skin like an open flame.

"Luke," he said, his voice low and gravelly. A spark of something she didn't want to acknowledge shimmied down her spine.

She had the right man. Luke Crandall. But that didn't quiet her rattled nerves.

Maybe because he didn't match what she'd imagined— an overweight chef who'd sampled too many sauces, kind of a warm, fuzzy, teddy-bear type. This man looked more like a grizzly, with a five-o'clock shadow accenting his powerful, square jaw. His dark, wavy hair stood out in all directions as if he'd wrestled a mountain lion. His taut muscles coiled and flexed with the slightest motion beneath a simple white T-shirt which made him seem too sexy for a chef...and far too dangerous for her.

Her wary gaze skimmed down his length, from those broad shoulders to his thin waist and narrow hips. His faded jeans had turned white at the knees and had frayed at the ends where they dusted his bare feet. He left an indelible impression on her: one Sydney deciphered as powerful awareness that had her wobbling in her high-heeled pumps. Her senses went on full alert.

"Miss Reede?"

Her gaze shot upward. Swallowing hard at the fact she'd been caught staring at him, she nodded.

"Sydney." Her voice came out a squeak. Swallowing back her hesitations, she said, "Did I catch you at a bad time?'' She glanced at her watch to be sure she was precisely on time, as usual. "I thought we said two o'clock?"

He rubbed a hand over his face. "It's two already?"

"Yes."

"I heard a car door slam. It woke me up. When I saw you coming up the walk, I thought..." His gaze flicked over her fresh linen suit in a measuring glance. Her insides squirmed. "I thought you were selling something. Like an Avon lady."

"Not quite." Unconsciously, she straightened her white blouse and took a step backward, ready to hire a caterer and forget trying to please her boss, the V.P. and Roxie before she stepped one foot in this man's house. "If you'd rather, I could come back later—"

"Now's fine." He glanced over his shoulder. "We said two o'clock." Again he lowered his voice, which sounded more and more like a growl with a touch of a Southern drawl. "I don't usually sleep through the afternoon. But it was a late night." He shrugged as if that explained everything. "Come on in." He pushed the door open wider.

Sirens wailed in her mind. She felt like an underrated actress in a B movie being invited into Dracula's castle as the audience screamed, "Don't go in!" Something didn't quite add up here. Was she missing part of the equation?

This man was a friend and past employer of Roxie's. Her friend wouldn't have hooked her up with a dangerous man. Some inner instinct, maybe her feminine core that burned with awareness, warned her Luke Crandall was more than she'd bargained for and far more dangerous than she could possibly imagine.

"A late night at your restaurant?" she asked, stalling.

"No. Emily kept me up." He frowned. "Again."

Emily? Roxie hadn't mentioned a wife or girlfriend. Was she stepping into the middle of a hot little tryst? She pursed her lips. She didn't care to know about his private life. "Maybe I should come back later."

"No." He reached for her, catching her wrist like a steel trap. Her stomach dropped. Her blood turned cold, then hot, the pressure of his fingers against her flesh making her heart pound. Automatically, she pulled back, but she couldn't have escaped him. Part of her didn't want to. The insane part, she decided.

"Let go." She tried to sound stronger and tougher than her wobbly knees made her feel. She stiffened her backbone and glared back at him.

"I need you." His voice cracked and shot down her defenses. She stared into his dark, almost black eyes and felt as if he'd swallowed her whole. A calming warmth settled over her. Her arm went slack, and he released her. She should have stepped away first, but she couldn't move. His hooded gaze entranced her.

He blinked and took a step back as if he'd suddenly realized what he'd done. "Sorry about that." His gaze dropped to the white bracelet the impression of his hand had made on her wrist. "Roxie said you could help."

"Not with your personal life. I'm an accountant, Mr. Crandall. Not a counselor."

Once again, his gaze skimmed over her, this time slower, making her blood simmer and her skin tighten. "You don't look like any accountant I ever saw."

She crossed her arms over her chest. "Looks can be deceiving. You don't look like a chef either."

"What'd you expect? The Pillsbury Doughboy?"

No, she thought. But she would have felt a whole lot safer and infinitely more relaxed.

If she thought he'd looked sexy before, she'd been completely wrong. When this man smiled, a ray of sunshine transformed his face, made his dark eyes burn like coal with a warmth that penetrated the shell she'd built around her heart. His white teeth looked even brighter against the dark stubble covering his jaw. He had a wide, generous mouth that softened the lines bracketing his lips and made her think of stolen kisses. She felt a blush radiate from deep inside her.

He laughed, a throaty sound that echoed off the entryway ceiling. His shoulders hunched forward suddenly as if the sound caused him pain. He bit out a curse word. "Here goes. One." He pointed a finger toward her. "Two." He added his middle finger. "Three." He closed his eyes tight.

A staccato cry started somewhere behind him. The baby's cry turned into a long wail. It set Sydney's nerves on fire.

"Come on in," he said, backing into his house. His walk turned into a run as he called over his shoulder, "I'll be right back." He disappeared into the darkness of his house, his bare feet slapping against the hardwood floors.

Stunned, Sydney remained on the porch. The baby's cry filled her mind. It pierced the walls of her heart that crumbled beneath the weight of her silent pain. She thought she'd put all that in the past, closing and locking that door.

She'd learned the hard way that only on her accounts at work did the numbers add up the way she liked. In real life, her debit column far exceeded the credits. To an accountant, that was unacceptable. To her womanly heart, life simply seemed unfair. Determined to even the score, she'd started a new life. She'd decided to have what most women with families and kids couldn't—a real career. She'd climb the corporate ladder as far as it would take her. Nothing would stop her.

Feeling more grounded, she watched Luke round the corner, jiggling a chubby baby in his arms. The little girl, dressed in a pink flowery jumper, had her father's dark, assessing eyes and wavy black hair. The crying had stopped, and Sydney heard a happy gurgle of delight. She watched this giant of a man wrestle a squirming baby from shoulder to shoulder. Her heart rolled over and crumbled like a clump of dirt. By the time he reached the open door, he was smiling, his eyes crinkling with pleasure. Her heart ached with a pain so intense her knees almost buckled.

Twisting the baby in his arms to face Sydney, he said, "This is Emily. Roxie said you might be able to offer some advice on raising kids if I helped you with cooking."

A rock-hard lump formed in her throat, and she forced it down with a determined swallow. "She did?"

"I thought she explained everything."

Apparently not. Suddenly the missing numbers in the equation appeared. Questions divided her thoughts and loyalties. Why hadn't Roxie told her? Did her friend know she wouldn't have come? Why couldn't Luke's wife help him? No, wait. She didn't want to know that answer. Frankly, she didn't want to know anything else about this sexy chef and his adorable daughter.

Picking up her bag of recipe books, she said in a formal, clipped tone, "I'm sorry, Mr. Crandall, there's been a mistake." She felt numb all over. "I can't help you with your baby."

His brow furrowed, erasing his smile, leaving a cold chill inside her. "You didn't help raise your brothers and sisters?" he asked. "Roxie said..."

Her knees weakened, but not her resolve. She wasn't a baby-sitter! She was an accountant. "Look, Mister Crandall—"

"Luke." He shifted his daughter in his arms, jiggling her up and down. The baby gurgled and cooed. Purposefully, Sydney shifted her gaze away from that sweet, slobbery smile and met Luke's hard gaze squarely with her own steely determination.

"Luke." She caught the quaver in her voice and frowned. "I-I don't know what all Roxie told you, but—"

He took a step forward, his shadow crossing her, making her forget her words. "She said you know kids."

"Did. Past tense. B-but I haven't been around any in a while." She remembered the sweet smell of holding her baby sister and the enthusiastic hugs of her younger brothers. Her resolve wavered. "My brothers and sister are all grown up now."

"You can't help me?" The lines in his face deepened, and the patches beneath his eyes darkened with defeat. A piece of her heart crumpled. "What'll I do now?"

She tried to bolster her resistance, but the despair in his voice, the pain in his eyes undermined her attempts. The same question echoed in her brain. If she didn't help him, then he might not help her. Her desperation felt like a shredded rope. Who else would she turn to for help with the shower? She didn't have time for a formal class. What could she do? Give up?

Hell, no. Sydney never gave up. Okay, she amended, rarely.

This was too important. Her whole career could be on the line. Well, that might be exaggerating things. But her racing pulse made her feel as if she was choosing between a career and an unemployment line. She'd simply have to shove aside her hesitations and do what had to be done. As if pushing up her sleeves for an unpleasant task, she squared her shoulders and swore to herself she wouldn't get emotionally involved with Luke or his daughter. She wouldn't let Luke's pained gaze get to her. And she wouldn't breathe in the scent of baby powder either.

She took a decisive step forward. She'd swoop in like Mary Poppins, accomplish what needed to be done, then soar back to her own life...alone. "I'll see what I can do."

Luke Crandall felt as if the cavalry bugled its *Charge* and galloped to his rescue. Relief rushed through him, trailed slowly by a twinge of guilt that nipped at his conscience.

So Sydney hadn't known the price of her cooking lesson. Why had Roxie kept it from her? He shrugged away his concerns. Roxie was too preoccupied with her impending mommyhood to remember minor details. It didn't matter now anyway. Sydney Reede was here. And he needed her help.

Balancing a cooing Emily on his shoulders, her little hands clutching his hair in a death grip, his hands bracketing her diapered hips and waist, he led Sydney through the disaster zone known as his house. It looked as if a tornado had roared through his living room. Caring for Emily had required more energy, more time, much more than he'd ever imagined. In the last week, he hadn't bothered to pick up her toys. Or anything else. He'd been too busy mopping up her messes.

"Uh, did Roxie tell you anything at all about Emily?" he asked, facing the woman. He tried to ignore the way her pink lips curled in an enticing way. But he couldn't ignore the jolt it gave his pulse. In her eyes, eyes that were wide and shockingly blue as a Texas summer day, he saw determination and a warmth that drew him like the seductive heat of the sun.

He cursed the fact that if he'd met Sydney two weeks ago he would have had the luxury of pursuing her. Not for a long-term relationship. That had never been his goal with women. But he did like the chase. Now, he didn't have the time or energy for even that. All because of Emily. The fact that he resented his tiny, sweet daughter's intrusion into his life rankled him, and he cursed himself for being a jerk.

"No." Sydney's voice sounded softer than her earlier crispness. "What was Rox supposed to tell me?"

"Nothing really. I thought she might have explained about this...emergency."

"I'm not a baby-sitter," she said matter-of-factly.

"No, no. You've got the wrong idea," he said, backpedaling. "See, Emily's mom...Sheila...my ex-girlfriend... uh, we were never married. She had Emily. Ten months ago."

Sydney's eyes widened, then narrowed. "That doesn't really constitute an emergency these days, Mister—"

"Luke. The emergency is…here. Now. I didn't know about the baby." He shook his head, still not believing the events that had transpired over the last few days. "Not till last week. We weren't together when she learned she was pregnant. Then Sheila decided to have the baby on her own."

"Why?" Sydney asked, startling him.

He shrugged, not totally understanding the reason himself. As a kid from a broken home, he knew the importance of a family. Or lack of one. He knew the heartache of not having a father, of a mother too self-absorbed with her own failures to focus on him. Sheila had never seemed the motherly type. She had certainly never been interested in marriage. He'd met her while she was visiting Dallas on business. He'd liked her independence, determination and drive. But mostly her distance.

His gaze narrowed on Sydney's butter-yellow linen suit and white no-nonsense blouse. She seemed the same corporate type. Why did Roxie think Sydney knew anything about babies? Before he agreed to this exchange of…uh-hum…services, he better find out her credentials.

"Emily's mom is a career gal, like yourself. Always on the upward move. I'm surprised she had the baby myself."

"I meant," Sydney said, the words coming slowly, her blue eyes turning as cold as a wintry sky, "why didn't she contact you…the father?"

"You're wondering how I know Em's mine," he said with a knowing smile. "I would have doubted…questioned the fact more closely, if Sheila wasn't one of the most honest, forthright women I've ever known. And except for the blatant fact that Em looks too much like me to deny it." He swung Emily down from her perch on his shoulders and cradled her in his arms. Turning her so she looked toward Sydney, he placed his cheek next to his daughter's.

Both of them grinned. Pride and love filled Luke's chest like a warm, gooey filling. "Don't you think?"

A strange glint darkened Sydney's eyes, made the corners of her mouth look strained. She swallowed, the muscles along the column of her throat tightening. "Yes."

"Look at this." He turned on his bare heel and grabbed a small black-and-white photograph off the mantel. Pride made his heart do a fast roll. "I found this the other night, after Emily had finally gone to sleep." The striking resemblance of brown, almost black wavy hair, even darker eyes and the same button nose still astounded, thrilled, awed him.

Sydney nodded. "I take it that's your bare bottom."

His gaze collided with hers. Heat surged through him. He coughed, feeling suddenly vulnerable. Had he detected a huskiness to her voice? Her words were flirtatious, but he swallowed a sexy comeback, one he might have used only weeks ago. He wasn't the same man anymore. His daughter had changed him...and his life.

Then he noticed Sydney's posture looked closed, almost aloof. Maybe she hadn't meant the comment as a come-on. His interest in her had been stirred up because he'd been locked in his house for almost a week. He felt like a caged animal. Guilt stalked him for blaming little Emily. It wasn't her fault. He blamed himself for being too much like his father.

"Well," he tried for a light tone, "if you offer to change Em's diaper, then you can check out the resemblance yourself."

"Diaper changing falls under a father's duties," she said in a clipped tone. "You need the practice."

His smile faded beneath the force of reality. Years of diaper changing, spoon-feeding strained peas and picking up, cleaning up, wiping up numerous messes and spills lay before him. The monotonous days, weeks and months seemed to pile on top of him, weighing him down under a blanket of suffocating responsibility.

Sydney's mouth curved into a delicious half grin that made him think of soft, slow kisses that could last half the night, and his body grew taut. She tempted him to chuck it all, to forget his responsibilities…like his dad.

Then Emily squealed. He punched himself mentally for even thinking of turning his back on his daughter. What kind of a father was he? He prayed he hadn't inherited any of his father's genes the way Emily had inherited his own looks.

Hooking his arm around her middle, he settled her against his side and wiggled her nose with his forefinger. "She may look like me, but that's where the similarities end." He put the picture back on the mantel. "Otherwise, I'm afraid she's like her mother. She likes to stay up half the night and wake up at the crack of dawn. Do you think her internal clock is still on East Coast time? And she's awfully finicky about what she eats. That's not like me at all."

"I thought chefs were very particular about what they ate," Sydney challenged him.

"I like food." He shrugged as he felt his spine stiffen rebelliously inside him. Immediately, he responded by putting up barriers against Sydney, for his daughter's sake. "All kinds of food. Em only likes cheese and plums."

"Was she on a special formula? Did her mother tell you any of that?"

"Yeah, she drinks that stuff twice a day. But she hates the cereal. I can't blame her for that. It looks like glue. She won't eat half the things Sheila said to try. I made an apple cobbler. It's a specialty at my restaurant. We have patrons that come back time and again just for the cobbler. So, I made the apple part without all the dough, hoping Em would eat it. But she turned up her nose at it."

"She's probably a little disoriented," Sydney explained. "Her world has been turned upside down."

So had his.

"It takes time."

"Maybe you're right." Of course, it would take time for his focus to shift from being a bachelor to that of a devoted father. "Sure," he added with more gusto and determination, "you're right." He sat on the arm of the sofa and held his daughter along the top of his thigh. She kicked her legs and squealed with glee. "Sheila didn't take a lot of time to explain things. She basically dumped Emily and left on the next plane out."

"That's terrible."

He shrugged. "It was my turn. She said she'd done her part. And she left Emily with me, the custodial papers signed and sealed."

"You never considered marriage?" she asked.

Surprised at her comment, he shook his head. "Not to someone I didn't love. I know that sounds awful, but Sheila felt the same way. A marriage without love wouldn't have been worth the cost of the license."

A twitch in Sydney's brow alerted him to her disapproval. But her calm, detached mask remained in place. She tugged on her short-cropped auburn hair, focusing his gaze on her slender neck that reminded him of Audrey Hepburn's trademark. Something about Sydney—maybe it was her heart-shaped face, her blazing hair that accented her delicate, pale features or her vivid blue eyes that shone like brilliant sapphires—made his stomach tighten. Was it anticipation or wariness? Should he stay away from this innocent-eyed beauty? Or should he try to get to know her?

Definitely not! He had more than he could handle right now. Between the constant demands of Emily and the restaurant, he barely had time for what little sleep he did manage.

Sydney's gaze lifted toward his daughter. Something in

her eyes softened, deepening the color, zapping the brightness he'd glimpsed earlier. "How long have you had Emily?"

"A week." When the baby gurgled, he jiggled her up and down, like he'd seen Uncle Charlie handle one of the triplets on *My Three Sons*. He'd seen a lot of old reruns this week while juggling Emily and a bottle in the middle of the night.

His daughter cooed and gave him a smile that melted his heart. *His daughter.* He never knew he could feel this fiercely, this protective, this connected to anyone. Each time he looked at her, he still felt awed. He could spend hours watching her tiny fingers curl around his, her mouth suckle a bottle, her eyes dancing with light. For a moment, the burden of responsibility lifted and his heart took flight.

"She seems happy and healthy. What else could you hope for?" Sydney held her bag close to her stomach, her knuckles as chalky as Emily's formula, and took a step back as if heading toward the door.

His pulse quickened. He couldn't let her leave. He needed her help. There were too many questions, too many unknowns in this Wonderland of diapers and lollipops. And Sydney seemed to have some of the answers he so desperately needed.

He set Emily in her playpen. Shoving his fingers through his hair, he paced in front of the mesh contraption, effectively blocking Sydney's escape route.

"I need help, Sydney," he said honestly, desperately. "I don't know what the hell I'm doing. I'm not qualified for changing diapers or...or late night feedings. I've got sole custody of a kid...my kid. I'm thirty-five, for God's sake! What do I know about babies? I'm too old, too set in my ways, and way too irresponsible." He shot her a sidelong glance. "So I've been told by a long string of ex-girlfriends."

"But not Emily's mother, right?" she asked.

He pressed the heels of his hands against his burning, bloodshot eyes and wished he could crawl back to bed for another twelve hours. Sleep was a faded memory. He hadn't had a full night's rest since...

Since Emily had arrived.

As if on cue, his ten-month-old daughter punched her fists into the air and started to wail. Her little face screwed up, her eyes squeezed shut. She was a cute kid...when she wasn't crying, spitting up or doing any of the other not-so-pleasant things babies did. Which, he'd discovered, was more than he'd ever imagined or wanted to know.

The headache he'd held at bay steamrolled over him, flattening his patience. "How the hell am I supposed to get the hang of this? I don't know what she wants...or needs. If only she could talk!"

Mostly, she cried and babbled in some gibberish that made him think he'd lost his mind. Maybe he had.

"Her lamb." Sydney smiled, really smiled. The brilliance of that smile shattered the last of Luke's composure. Simultaneously, he wanted to curse her and kiss her. What did she find so damn funny? Emily's cries acted like knife pricks down his spinal column. But at the same time, he noticed the seductive slant of Sydney's mouth, the slow curve of her bottom lip and the shimmer of gloss. His powerful attraction to her knocked the wind out of him.

"She wants her lamb." A hint of laughter lilted her voice.

Dumbstruck, Luke could only stare at her.

Sydney knelt and picked up the lamb outside of the playpen and plunked it into Emily's arms. "See? She's happy now."

"I knew Roxie was right. You know kids."

Her eyes narrowed. "That didn't require calculus to figure out."

"But you raised your siblings, right?"

"Helped." She glanced sideways toward Emily. "I was

nine going on twenty when my mom died. My baby sister, Jennie, was younger than your daughter. And my two or-nery brothers were still in diapers. So, I guess you could say, I got an early start on Big Bird and bottles.''

So much for his concern about her qualifications. He started pacing again. He wished he'd had brothers or sisters. He didn't know anything about babies, except what he'd learned in a crash course over the last week. "There's so much I don't know. Like, does she sleep enough? Is she getting enough to eat?" He raked his fingers through his hair. Questions zinged around his head like a Ping-Pong ball. "Should I have beer in the fridge? Could she get to it? Would that be dangerous? Should I throw out the swim-suit issue of *Sports Illustrated?* Will it give her warped ideas? What about—''

''Whoa,'' Sydney said, her smile widening. "It'll be some time before you have to worry about boyfriends and dating and how to pay for the wedding.''

He felt the blood drain out of his head.

She laughed, the sound rippling through the room like a string of bells. The tension around her mouth and eyes eased. Her engaging smile dimpled her cheeks and punched a hole in his gut. As his body became uncomfortably warm with a sudden attraction, hers seemed to relax, her shoul-ders releasing as she let her bag slide to the floor.

Feeling as if he'd just missed catching the "Hail Mary" pass at the end of the SuperBowl, he sank onto the arm of the sofa again. "I'm worrying about too much already, huh?''

She gave him a friendly wink. "Maybe just a little. Par-enting isn't a list of do's and don'ts.''

''There's not a handbook that everyone's hiding from me?''

''Nope. I don't think you could put all the things you'd need to know about parenting in the Smithsonian.''

He rubbed his jaw, felt the bristles scratch his palm.

Glancing at Sydney, he suddenly felt rumpled and disheveled. When had he last shaved? A woman like Sydney, all dressed up for a cooking lesson, probably liked *GQ*-type men. Then he kicked himself mentally. What did he care what Sydney thought of the way he dressed or how he'd forgotten to shave that morning? He only needed her advice on babies...not fashion. He certainly wasn't looking for her approval or even a date.

Shifting mental gears back to his more significant problems, he said, "You're saying it's more than I can learn."

She stepped toward him and placed a gentle hand on his shoulder. "Not at all."

Her touch heated his blood instead of soothing his concerns. She made him think of cool moonbeams on a hot summer night. Things he probably shouldn't be thinking with his daughter in the same room. Restraining his sudden interest in this woman, like a leash on a wild beast, he shifted his gaze toward Emily and focused on his baby. His daughter sat on her diapered bottom, her pudgy legs out in front of her, as she gnawed on the lamb's ear. She was the most important female in his life now.

"You're feeling all the natural things a parent fears and worries about," Sydney said, her voice smooth as satin sheets. "You can't know it all. There's too many unknown factors. Face it, you're going to make mistakes. Your parents did. Mine did. And we all survived."

Did we? Had he really come out of the so-called family unit unscathed? He didn't want to think about that. He promised himself he wouldn't put Emily through the same nightmare.

"You don't sound much like an accountant." Warily, he eyed her. She'd tapped into his thoughts and fears and hesitations.

"Like I said, looks are deceiving." Her gaze shifted toward the place she touched, as if she only now realized it. A sizzle of electricity vibrated between them, singed the air around them. As quick as a lightning flash, she pulled her hand away.

Walking to the other side of the playpen, she put distance between herself and Luke. "You've got time to figure out what you think is best for your daughter. Talk to other parents. I'm sure there are a zillion clubs you can join. Support groups, even. I certainly don't know all the answers either."

"But you said you helped raise your brothers and sister?" he pulled out his last piece of hope.

Her delicate features seemed to freeze. She shuttered her emotions behind dark lashes. "I did. And they've all turned out well. But I can't take the credit. My dad was pretty amazing."

"But *you* helped."

"Yes, I did."

"Then you could help me. Temporarily. Until I get on my feet...get this parenting thing down to a fine art."

"Well, I don't have that much time." She flashed him a smile that just as quickly vanished.

"I won't take up much. Maybe a couple of nights here and there. If you'd be available for when I have a question. Like if she chokes. If she gets a fever. If she eats dirt."

Sydney's smile tightened with barely restrained exasperation. "Call 9-1-1. Take an emergency aid course. Learn the Heimlich. Otherwise, call the doctor. And remember, dirt won't hurt her."

After a week of feeling isolated and alone, he needed someone to discuss his situation with. He needed answers to his questions. He couldn't take no for an answer. "Of course, we'll have to spend some time together to help with *your* project." He let that sink in with her. Her gaze slanted toward him. Slowly, her shoulders twisted until she faced him again. "Some of the time could easily overlap."

Crossing her arms over her chest, she took the stance of an interrogator. "Roxie said you're an excellent chef."

It was a statement, but he heard the doubt in her husky tone. He swallowed any modesty he usually doled out. He had to impress the socks off this woman, make her think he was the *only* chef who could help her. "I've won several awards. I don't pretend to be a typical chef. But then I never have to defend my cooking. What kind of cuisine are you trying to learn?"

"A variety, but mostly French. Like chocolate soufflé and crème brûlée."

"French, huh?" He gulped, trying to hide his concern. He scratched his jaw. "Uh-huh." He knew French fries, French onion soup, French bread and a few bawdy French wines, but he wouldn't call himself an expert of the caliber of Julia Child. Maybe he could come up with a new variety of French cuisine...maybe vegetarian chili with a croissant on the side. But who'd buy it?

"Are *you* qualified?" She tossed his concern back at him.

He'd based his reputation on the hottest chili north of the Rio Grande, the devil-may-care kind. He called his brew-pub the Iron-horse Brewery, because customers had to have a cast-iron stomach to handle the spicy chili and robust beer. But he'd also created a warm apple cobbler and a dessert he'd named the chocolate meltdown that made most women salivate.

Why not French cuisine?

"But of course," he stated in his worst imitation accent. He hid his doubts behind a jaunty smile. *"Oui, mademoiselle."*

Chapter Two

A career gal like you.

The simple statement, more like an accusation, still rang in Sydney's mind two days later at work. She hadn't denied the comparison Luke had made between her and his ex…whatever. Although she knew it wasn't exactly true. Baby Emily's mother had been able to have what Sydney couldn't—her very own baby. A chasm opened inside her, the empty space throbbing with an irrepressible ache. How could that woman have given her child up as if Emily were a worn-out turntable?

Shuffling through a stack of papers on her desk, she knew there was no true comparison between herself and Emily's mother. She figured Luke's hasty assumption was easier to digest than the dreaded question she'd grown to hate—"How come a pretty girl like you isn't married with two kids?" It was always meant, she supposed, as a compliment, but it felt like a knife slicing through her hopes, shredding her dreams all over again.

She'd been given a chance at pseudomotherhood with her siblings. Yet, she'd been denied the chance to have children of her own. The biting reality had crushed her spirit, her hope, her life. But not anymore. After years of trying, then facing the painful truth, she'd given up that dream and refocused her life. On her career. That was her baby now.

Her chest tightened. She knew it would never truly replace the feel of a warm, soft, cuddly baby nestled in her arms. But she couldn't do anything about that now. She certainly didn't have to dwell on the impossible. Concentrating on her career helped her make it through each long, empty day...alone.

"Good morning."

Glancing up, Sydney stuffed her emotions back into the hidden spaces of her heart and managed a smile at Roxie, who'd stopped beside her cubicle. The expectant mother arched her back, making her round belly extend even further. Uncomfortable staring at that huge stomach, Sydney focused again on the papers, filing through the stack as if she'd struck out on a mission. It didn't feel like a good morning. Inside Sydney, it felt overcast with a hundred percent chance of rain. Blinking back those tears she'd thought had disappeared months ago, she managed, "Is it?"

"What's wrong?" Roxie hitched her hip on the edge of her desk. "Didn't the meeting with Luke go well?"

"Oh, that. Yeah, I guess so."

"Then what?"

Sydney rubbed at the frown pinching her brow. "Just worried about my little sister. How could I have raised her? Me, an accountant. She is so irresponsible with money. Again, she went over her budget and is calling for help. And what will I do?"

"Bail her out, of course."

Sydney gave a wry grin. It was another reason she wanted...needed this promotion. She'd offered to pay her little sister's tuition. But the expenses kept adding up, multiplying. "You know me too well."

Roxie nodded. "Yep. And I know how much you love Jennie. She's young. She's in college. She'll learn."

"If I have to beat it into her stubborn head."

Roxie chuckled. "So enough stalling. I want to hear the good stuff. What'd you think?"

"About?" The numbers in front of her blurred.

"Luke. Luke Crandall, remember?"

She shrugged. "Oh, he was all right. Nice enough."

"All right? Nice? You didn't think he was gorgeous?"

Sydney rolled her eyes. "If you like the tall, dark and sexy type."

"Nope, I'd rather have the short, fat and bald type myself." Roxie fanned herself then leaned forward as much as her stomach would allow. A gleam made her eyes shine like foil in the sun. "You thought he was sexy?"

"I didn't say—"

"Yes, you did." She rocked back with a satisfied smirk.

"I'm not interested in any man." Sydney was more than a little tired of this worn-out conversation. "I'm a career gal."

Roxie's brow furrowed. "Did y'all work out a deal?"

As if her friend's baby held a magnet for Sydney's gaze, she watched Roxie's hand move over the rounded surface. At least she'd never have to worry about getting her figure back after swelling up like she'd swallowed a watermelon seed. A memory of Luke smiling and holding his baby flashed in her mind. He'd been so proud of the resemblance between himself and his daughter—his little piece of immortality. A familiar ache resonated inside her chest, but she ignored it.

"How are you feeling?" she asked Roxie.

"Like I was due three months ago." She waved her finger and tsked. "Answer my question."

"Are you playing boss now?"

"I'm your friend, Sydney." She placed a hand on her shoulder. "I know I've put you in a bind with this shower."

Sydney shook her head, denying the truth.

"I'm responsible. So, tell me what y'all decided."

Knowing she couldn't dance around the topic, Sydney puffed out an exasperated breath, lifting her wispy bangs off her forehead. "We're making dessert tonight."

"Hot damn." Roxie's eyes widened at her own raised voice, and she laughed, throwing her head back with delight.

Sydney put a finger to her pursed lips. "Keep it down. I didn't say we were making wild, passionate love."

"Well, I can hope, can't I?"

Sighing, Sydney sat back in her chair. "You're incorrigible. I've given up on men. I don't have time for them." She swiveled her chair back to face her computer screen. "The only thing cooking between Luke and me is whatever's on the stove."

"Sure." Roxie shook her head. "You're married to work."

"Exactly." But Sydney knew instinctively she'd felt a spark, a sizzle, a slow burn between her and Luke. The idea terrified her. Why would she want another relationship, where she'd eventually have to admit her inability to have children, see pity in his dark eyes, then feeling a coolness fill the space between them? Why would she want to feel inadequate all over again? It wasn't worth the heartache, the possibility of rejection. She'd rather be alone. Here, in her office cubicle, her inability to have kids didn't matter. Here, she felt safe, in control.

With Luke, she didn't think the shimmy of anticipation would fizzle any time soon. He was sexy. She'd have to rely on his daughter to douse the spark of attraction with a cold reality. Sydney had already raised three kids that weren't her own. She wasn't exactly sure what Luke expected out of their trade, but she wouldn't raise somebody else's kid again. If that's what he had in mind, then she'd squelch that plan quick. Even if her heart cried for the motherless little girl and her eye roamed toward the sexy but overwhelmed father.

In between feeding, changing and rocking Emily, Luke studied the cookbooks Sydney had left. No wonder the woman hadn't been able to cook. She was trying to do it like a Betty Crocker cake recipe. Real gourmet cooking required a piece of the soul and a touch of inspiration. Having the basic idea in his head, he decided he'd improvise. As always.

"How'd you like Sydney?" Roxie asked over the phone later that Monday afternoon.

"You sure she knows kids?" he asked, jiggling Emily and cradling the receiver against his ear and shoulder.

"Yeah, why?"

"She didn't seem too taken with my daughter."

Roxie laughed. "Maybe she was overwhelmed by you."

He maneuvered the phone with his jaw and wiped more drool off his daughter's chin with a dish towel. "What do you mean?"

"Could she have been smitten by a certain handsome bachelor? You know how women find men and babies irresistible."

"No, I didn't know. Should I cart Em to a singles bar?" Roxie laughed.

Then her words fueled an idea. "Seems odd though. I feel like I've played chicken with a semi. And lost." He sniffed the shirt he'd had on since Sunday, the one he'd slept in, the one spotted with baby food and drool. He figured he better shower and change before Sydney arrived this evening. "I doubt she was interested in me or Emily."

Remembering Sydney's cautious smile and tentative agreement, he knew he had to pull out all the stops. He'd start with wine, get the lady to relax, take her mind off cooking. He should know how to distract a woman! If he got her and kept her interested in him, then maybe she wouldn't notice any blunders he might make on the stove. He'd use his tried-and-true method of seduction, add in a few flashy techniques with utensils to let her see he knew his way around a kitchen and let her sample a succulent dessert. He'd decided to make his special chocolate meltdown, but he had to make it sound more French. Maybe chocolate éclair with a flair? He cringed at his own bad accent.

Then he'd have her right where he wanted her. She'd be putty in his hands, more than willing to teach him the fine art of parenting. After all, how long could it take to figure out a few desserts for a bunch of women? With that behind them, they'd concentrate on his more immediate concerns—caring for Emily.

"Trust me, there won't be anything cooking over here but what's in the oven. You know anything about French cuisine?"

"Nope," Roxie said. "I had a good bottle of wine once. Come to think of it, that's how I ended up pregnant." She laughed. "Must've been more potent than I thought."

"I'll keep that in mind. I don't want any more surprises." He handed Emily her stuffed lamb. "Sydney doesn't seem the type to be interested in a single father." He glanced under the kitchen table and behind a cereal box. "I'm not looking for anything except Emily's pacifier."

"Uh-huh."

She hung up, letting Luke doubt his own words. He could admit to himself that Sydney Reede had caught his attention, hook, line and sinker. What man wouldn't have been attracted to her? It was natural. It was stupid.

Emily started to fuss, and he began singing her favorite song, the only one that seemed to soothe her. He reminded himself that he had no room in his life for a woman like Sydney. Emily had turned his world topsy-turvy. He didn't need to create a whirlwind of confusion by falling in love.

Although, he admitted, a good baby-sitter would be welcome.

She'd arrived precisely on time.
He'd been late.
Now, thirty minutes later, after she'd unloaded her supplies for baklava, Sydney grew tired of waiting for Luke to put his daughter to bed. She slipped off her work pumps and tiptoed down the hall. What was keeping him?

Earlier, the baby had cried that frustrated, red-in-the-face attempt to battle the sleep bandit. Sydney had resisted going to Luke's aid. He had to learn to cope. She wouldn't let him depend on her in any way. Because she sure wasn't sticking around after the baby shower. They'd agreed to work together on baklava and babies over the next month. But that was all.

A pale light fell across the beige carpet and a low rumbling sound greeted her as she reached the nursery. She peered into the darkened room and saw Luke swaying back and forth in a creaking rocker with Emily contentedly tucked against his broad shoulder. In the shadowy corner of the room, an avalanche of diapers spilled out over the cardboard box they'd come in. Toys littered the floor like a mob scene at Santa's workshop.

Staying in the shadows, she watched Luke, his wide, tan hand patting his daughter's little back in a slow, soothing motion. He sang something that sounded like a lullaby, but his voice was too deep, too rusty to understand the words. The tender scene tweaked Sydney's heartstrings. Leaning her head against the doorjamb, she wondered what it would be like to have a husband doting on their baby. The thought stung her chest. Tipping her head back, she blinked back those damn threatening tears.

What was it about this house that made her want to cry all the time? She liked her life just the way it was. She didn't need a husband or a baby to make her feel complete.

Snatches of Luke's song sank into her thoughts—something about a tattoo and blaming a woman. It snagged her attention. Definitely not Brahms's Lullaby. Curious, she stuck her head further into the room. His gaze met hers, and the song died on his lips which curled in a you-caught-me grin.

"What are you doing?" she asked in a hushed tone.

"Singing my daughter to sleep." He spoke in the same tempo and rhythm of the song and continued rocking.

Sydney walked across the plush carpeted room, carefully stepping over plastic blocks and a fuzzy-eared lamb, and stopped in front of the rocker. Bending down, she studied Emily's sweet little face, her long silky lashes shading her pink cheeks, her moist lips parting slightly with each breath. Lifting the baby's fisted hand, she let it plunk back down against Luke's shoulder. "She's out all right. Probably for a while."

"All night?" Hope made his dark eyes gleam.

"No promises," she said. "You ought to know that by now."

"Do I ever." He leaned his head back against the rocker. "Do they ever sleep through the night?"

"Ah, the age-old question." She offered a sympathetic smile to ease his haggard face. "Some do. Some don't."

"Great. What do I do for sleep?"

"How about coffee?"

He frowned. "For how long?"

"Better get used to it. You'll survive off a caffeine high when she starts dating, staying out late with some high school boy who's driving her around, one wrist on the wheel, the other around your daughter's shoulders." A smile tugged at her mouth.

"You're getting a big laugh over this, aren't you?" he asked, his voice carrying a rusty quality that stirred something deep inside Sydney. He groaned and shifted Emily higher on his shoulder. Her little head lifted and bobbled like her neck was attached to a spring. She blinked then collapsed against his shoulder again, her heavy breathing loud in the stillness of the room. Luke released a held breath and brushed a tender kiss against the top of Emily's downy head. Sydney's heart turned over at the tender scene of father and daughter.

"Is she awake?" he asked.

Unable to speak, a lump of awe, regret and pain lodging in her throat, Sydney shook her head.

"Now what?" he asked.

She straightened, too aware of his masculine appeal, along with the soft smells of baby lotion and formula lingering on his skin. She refused to give in to his charm and the baby's sweetness. She had to keep her distance. Motioning toward the crib, she said, "Put her down."

"I'm stuck."

"Stuck?" Her brows slanted into a frown as she shifted to look at his narrow hips along the seat of the rocker. "Looks okay to me."

Silence radiated in the room like the warm glow of a fire. It caught in her cheeks, burning the realization of her blunder into her. She could have kicked herself. She tried not to glance at Luke but couldn't help but notice his smirk.

"Still as cute as my baby picture?" he asked.

She ignored him. "Just stand up and put her in the crib."

"What if I wake her?"

"You won't."

"I've done it before."

She let out an exasperated sigh. Time was wasting. What about her cooking lesson? Before she thought the whole thing through, she reached for the baby. Then it was too late.

Her hand brushed Luke's broad shoulder. She felt his heat, his strength, the way his muscles flexed in response to her touch. Her stomach clenched. Her gaze met his, locked, and a potent current as if from an electrical storm surged through her, shocking her senses awake. She should have backed away then, encouraged him to handle Emily himself, but that would have made her reaction to him too obvious. And she didn't want to acknowledge the dizzying anticipation that took hold of her and made her knees rubbery. With Roxie's prediction ringing in her ears, she decided to prove her friend wrong.

Focusing on the baby, she wiggled her hand between Luke's chest and the baby's belly and scooped the sleeping Emily into her arms. Without a glance in his direction, without sniffing the sweet smell of Emily, Sydney settled the baby in the crib and pulled a soft blanket over her pudgy body.

Stepping away, she could still feel the baby's soft form nestling against her in that brief second. The bittersweet imprint made her chest tighten with longing.

She felt heat along her right side and jumped. Startled by the realization that Luke stood behind her, not touching her, but too close for comfort, she felt trapped between his sweet-smelling daughter and his very real, very overwhelming maleness. Lured by confusing circumstances and caught by a biting reality, she felt her heart thunder. She should have never come here. She wished she could run like a coward. But her own powerful need locked her in place.

"I'm impressed." His voice felt like a silken caress against her ear and sent a shiver of pleasure down her spine. "You handled her like a pro. Ever thought of having your own?"

The heat he'd aroused in her suddenly diffused, leaving a cold, aching emptiness. She forced down the constricting lump in her throat. "No. I already raised three kids. Isn't that enough for any person?"

Fleeing the room as if a phantom chased her, she sensed Luke following her, her heartbeat quickening. Eager to distract her thoughts and gain control of the conversation, she asked, "What were you singing when I came in?"

He chuckled and rubbed his hand along his firm jaw. "Margaritaville."

She cut her eyes toward him.

He shrugged and grinned. "It was the only song I could think of. Em can't understand the words." He came to a dead halt and put a hand on her arm. She felt a tingling start in the pit of her stomach and ripple outward to her limbs. "Can she?"

His uncertainty made him even more attractive than she cared to admit. She found herself laughing. It struck her as odd that this man had already made her laugh in the short time she'd known him, when she hadn't managed to find anything to smile about for a very long while. "Don't worry. I'm sure she doesn't know what a tattoo is...or even a shaker of salt."

His shoulders slumped forward with relief. "Guess I'll have to learn some nursery rhymes and lullabies soon."

Again, she gave a bittersweet smile at his eagerness to learn all he needed to know to help his daughter. It made her heart swell then contract. Little Emily was a lucky baby. "She'll probably teach them to you when she goes to day care or if you hire a nanny or whatever you plan to do with her while you work. I'm sure your restaurant takes up a lot of time."

"It does. And I've been neglecting it. I'm sort of torn about what to do, how to handle all of this."

Here it comes, she thought, the request she'd been dreading. Hadn't she already made herself plainly understood? She wasn't a baby-sitter, temporary nanny or fill-in mom.

"I took Em to the restaurant the other night. She loved it. But it's really not the place for a young child. And I wasn't able to get much work done." His eyebrow lifted in question. "Maybe you'd like to go with us some time."

"I don't think so," she hedged, squaring her shoulders, readying herself for making a stand. Undermining her resistance was an overwhelming desire to see Luke's restaurant, to spend time with him. Reality squeezed her heart. He wasn't asking her out on a date. He only wanted a baby-sitter!

"What about your parents? Grandparents make great baby-sitters." She tipped the conversation back into his court.

"Not mine. Besides, they're always traveling. They didn't have time for me as a kid. I don't think they'd make Emily a top priority either." His voice dipped with sadness and made her heart ache for him.

She might have lost her mother at an early age, but her father had always been there for her. He'd held her tight when she'd crawled back home facing a divorce. He'd supported her decision to move to Dallas. She couldn't imagine not growing up with that kind of love and support.

"Have you looked into a good day care?" she asked.

"Yeah. None are open when I need to work. The restaurant biz has weird hours that don't necessarily coincide with raising a kid."

"You could hire a nanny," she offered.

"I thought of that. But..."

"What?"

"Then I'd be like my parents, handing Emily off to someone else to raise." He glanced down at the floor, and the lines around his mouth deepened. "I know there are good people out there, doing a great service, but I think it's the parents' responsibility. Quality time is one thing. But quantity speaks volumes to kids. At least it did to me."

Her heart constricted like a vise, and disappointment pressed through her veins. So he didn't want her to baby-sit. Why should she be upset by that? She wasn't. Or was she?

Okay, she admitted, it bothered her. Frankly, it pierced a vulnerable piece of her heart. Or maybe she simply admired him for trying to do the right thing. She realized then he wouldn't want her hanging around after their agreement ended. Which was fine with her. "Your stance is admirable. But unrealistic."

"Maybe. Only time will tell." He gave her a grin that melted the chill surrounding her heart. "So, you know any of those nursery rhymes?"

"Start with Eensy Weensy Spider," she said in an off-handed way. "Kids love those little hand gestures."

As if he took mental notes, he nodded, his features serious. "What happens after the rain washes the spider out? That was my favorite part…as a kid."

"Of course." Again, she laughed. This time, it felt good, really good…too good. Her smile faded. "The sun comes out."

"Kind of a parallel for life, huh?"

"Sometimes," she said, "sometimes not." Feeling the back of her eyes burn, she turned the corner at the end of the hall, leaving Luke behind as she headed for the kitchen.

When he caught up with her, he clapped his hands and rubbed his palms together, as if diffusing the cloud of gloom she'd brought upon herself. He gave her a jaunty smile. "I'm hungry. Have you eaten?"

Startled by his question, she leaned against the tiled island. "Uh, no, not really."

"Good. I thought we'd make this chocolate…well, it's like an éclair…sort of, but I call it a melt…ing…" His voice faded as he floundered. "It's a new dessert I'm working on for the restaurant." He frowned at her sharpening gaze.

"I thought this was my cooking lesson."

"It is."

She turned toward two grocery sacks on the counter. "I brought all these ingredients with me."

"Okay." He offered a congenial half smile. "What are we making? A soufflé? Cream broo…la…la?"

"You mean, crème brûlée?"

He snapped his fingers. "Exactly. Excellent. That was a

test." Coughing, he turned away and grabbed a bottle of
red wine from a rack above his refrigerator. Using a brass
corkscrew, he pulled out the cork. Mesmerized by the tight
movement of muscle play beneath his T-shirt, she stared at
him, like a silly schoolgirl with a crush. "A nice Beaujolais
will prepare our palates. Or do you want a beer instead?"

"No margaritas?" she joked.

"Good idea." He winked. Her stomach flip-flopped.
"I'm all out of tequila though. Next time."

Next time? How many next times would there be? Only
a month full, she reminded herself.

"Shouldn't we get started?"

"Right. Okay, crème—"

"No. Baklava."

His frown deepened. "That's Greek, right?"

"I guess."

"Hmm." He rubbed his chin.

"Can't you handle Greek cuisine?"

"Not a problem." He reached for the bottle of wine.
"Let's have a glass first, while I think about this." He
poured the wine with a flourish, twisting his wrist to save
a drop along the bottle's lip. He handed her a balloon glass
of the warm, burgundy liquid. "Remember, never rush
when cooking. That's when you make mistakes. Relax. Enjoy yourself."

At his encouragement, she lifted her glass to her lips.
But he stopped her from sipping with a hand on hers. His
hand was warm, rough, rugged. Her skin tightened as a
rippling heat wave burned its way up her arm and down
her spine.

"Wait," he said, his voice a hushed whisper that made
her toes curl. His shadowy gaze darkened as he stared at
her mouth. Silly, she chided herself, he was probably looking at the wine, probably saw a piece of cork floating in it.

"What?" she asked, impatient, nervous with him touching her, watching her so intensely, so intimately. She felt his warm, spearmint breath waft across her cheek.

"Swirl it first." He moved her hand and glass together in a slow, undulating motion between them. "Now breathe."

She couldn't. Not with him so close she could have lifted her face and kissed him. She didn't dare draw a breath. Not that she could have if she'd tried. Her chest ached, but not from any pain she'd ever known. This was a building pressure...like anticipation...and she realized with horror that she *wanted* Luke to kiss her.

"What's it like?" he asked, his voice an intimate whisper.

Her pulse pounded. "What?"

"The bouquet. What do you smell?"

You. His musky odor of pure male...and something else, something subtle, something intriguing, assaulted her senses. She sniffed the glass obediently and managed, "Wine."

With the patience of a wise teacher, he swirled the glass once more. "Try again."

"It's not wine?" she asked, her humor dry as her womb.

"Tell me more," he prodded.

This time, she managed a deeper breath. Ah, baby powder. She detected the lingering scent on the warmth of his skin. It was an odd combination that unnerved her.

"Is it sweet?" He leaned closer and drew in a deep breath, and his broad chest expanded, capturing her gaze. Beneath the white T-shirt, she saw the dusty swirls of dark hair across his chest, following the curve of his muscle which tapered into a slope that led down to the flat plane of his stomach.

She swallowed a groan. "Luke—"

"There's no right or wrong answer. Everyone detects something different. I want you to notice, to be aware of what your senses are telling you."

Believe me, I am. Too much so.

"I smell fermented grapes," she offered, hoping to end this mild form of torture.

He frowned. So, there had been a wrong answer. But he didn't press her further. He tipped the glass against her mouth. "Taste it."

Closing her eyes, she took a sip. The smooth, fruity flavor rolled over her tongue and down her throat. She felt a warmth flow outward from her center. She wasn't sure if it was the wine or Luke. She preferred to think it was the alcohol.

"Look, Luke." She moved a safe distance away and buttoned her suit jacket. "Let's get busy...cooking. I-I've got a meeting first thing in the morning. And I'd like to get to bed...early." *Wrong thing to say.* She paused, confused, her mind in a fog. "I'm just here to cook. That's all."

"I thought we were," he said in a sexy tone that made her tremble. "Actually that was lesson number one."

"And what was I supposed to learn from that?" she asked, uncomfortable with his teaching technique and more irritated at her own reaction than with Luke.

"That food...and drink, whether it be water, wine or iced tea, should be enjoyed, savored, not gulped. Same for cooking. It's an experience. Not an exercise." He poured himself a glass, but didn't bother swirling or sniffing before gulping.

"I just want—"

"I know what you want." He set the glass on the counter. The warmth left his gaze, leaving his eyes chilling, like a dark, winter night.

"You think cooking only requires step one, two, three." He snapped his fingers in rapid succession. "Then voilà. A soufflé. It doesn't work that way, lady. As it is, there are only a few truly great chefs. If you want to wow your guests then it's going to take time and patience. Otherwise, get a box cake and follow the directions on the back.

"That's why," he continued after wetting his whistle again, "the French know how to cook so well. It's an art to them. Just like painting, sculpting…making love. Aren't the French experts in love and romance?"

She blinked, her heart clattering. Heat poured through her veins like a hundred percent proof. "I've been to Paris. They have a lot of museums but not one for making love."

He scowled at her. "It permeates everything they do." He took a step closer, and she crossed her arms over her chest. "Sometimes you want the fast food variety. Fast and hot." She pressed her back against the center island, once more trapped, this time by him and her inability to run. "But that's all it is. It doesn't satisfy the body or nourish the soul. Does it?"

He took her glass, his fingers brushing hers, tickling her nerve endings, and filled it close to the brim. "Then again, if you take it slow." He slid the cool glass along her forearm, and a shiver arced through her. "Really slow. Until your senses explode from hunger and need," he said, his voice deep and dusty and only a breath away. "Then you'll know how to…" his hooded gaze made her blood pump hot and fierce "…cook."

Her breath whooshed out of her. She put a hand to her throat and felt her pulse skittering beneath her fingertips. "Luke—"

He moved away from her, crossed the kitchen and started rummaging through the cabinets, pulling out bowls, a sifter, measuring spoons. Metal clanged against metal as her heart kicked against her breastbone. What was happening to her?

What the hell was in that wine? Luke wondered. Roxie'd warned him of its potency. Had it gone to his head? Or had Sydney? He covered his own nerves by making more noise than necessary. Right now, he didn't care if Emily woke up and cried the rest of the night. At least he'd be rescued from himself and his attraction to Sydney.

He'd meant to flirt, tease, keep Sydney off center, especially when she'd pulled the rug out from under him and decided to make baklava this evening. But he was the one grasping for the equilibrium of reality. His plan to distract her had backfired. He'd gotten a little carried away, staring into her eyes that reminded him of plump blueberries, breathing in her tempting fragrance of Chanel No. 5, if he wasn't mistaken. And he rarely was.

"Maybe I should have stayed in the kitchen during my marriage," she said, stopping his clatter. He turned, saw her wide, expressive eyes, the wildfire of embarrassment burn her cheeks. "I-I can't believe I said that."

She turned away. Silence pounded in his ears.

"It's probably the wine," he offered. And more than likely his fault. He continued sorting through bowls as if selecting the perfect one. "So, you were married," he said, grasping another way to distract her without affecting himself this time. "Roxie didn't tell me."

"No reason she should have. It's over."

"You don't sound like a supporter of the institution."

She shrugged as if it hadn't mattered. But her eyes told a different story. One of pain. Or was it regret? "I guess it could work for some people. Just not for me and my ex."

Not for Luke either, not after surviving his parents' marriage. "How come?" Knowing he'd probably overstepped the thin boundary between them, but hoping she'd distract them both from this simmering attraction by some real-life consequences, he added, "You can tell me it's none of my business."

Drawing a shaky breath, she shook her head. "You were open with me about you and Emily's mom." She took another sip of wine, and he kept his gaze off her mouth and her long sleek neck as she swallowed. Heck, he yanked open a drawer and dug out a spatula that he didn't need. "I guess it all boiled down to compromise," she said. "We couldn't. And you can't have a successful marriage without it."

His dad hadn't been able to compromise either. He wondered if Sydney's all-important career had stood between her and her ex. That helped Luke gain control of his libido. For a long moment, he remained silent. When the minute dragged into two then three, he refilled his glass of wine and took a slow, deep swallow. He relished the warmth sliding into his belly, easing the questions, releasing the tension.

"So, that was lesson one, huh?" she asked.

"Too much for one night? Or are you ready for lesson number two?" Again, he couldn't smother his suggestive tone.

"I'm game if you are."

He almost choked on his surprise. Once again a current of attraction rippled between them. He'd taught himself not to play with fire. But this time, he couldn't seem to stop himself.

Chapter Three

"How long till she's housebroken?"

Sydney stifled her laughter. "You mean, potty trained?"

His nose pinched and features strained, Luke plunked a diaper in what he called the nuclear waste dump. The plastic lid closed with a snap. "Whatever."

Emily had woken up, crying and fussing, after they'd put the baklava in the oven. Luke had thought his daughter was hungry. But Sydney had known better. Maybe it was well-honed instincts or simply common sense. After all, the baby had had a full bottle right before she fell asleep in her daddy's arms. Physiology was the name of this early game of guess-what-your-baby-needs.

"So how long until...?"

"As soon as *you* train her."

"Can I start tomorrow?" He hefted Emily onto his shoulder, his large hands easily spanning her little waist.

"Maybe not quite that soon. Usually babies are potty trained anywhere from a year and a half to four years of age."

"Four!" Emily jerked at his loud voice, and he brought his voice down to a controlled whisper. "You mean she could be four and I'd still be changing her diaper?"

"Well, that's not college age." Laughter bubbled out of Sydney's throat. Curious, Emily turned her chocolate-brown eyes on Sydney. Luke held his daughter against his shoulder as the baby pumped her arms and stuck a fist out as if she wanted to shake hands. Sydney caught the plump little fist in her hand. The soft, tender skin brought a wave of memories and suppressed emotions. Sydney remembered playing "house" with her baby sister. It had helped to cope with her mother's death. It had brought moments of peace and serenity to what otherwise felt like a chaotic world to Sydney. She released that tiny hand, as if she had given up the idea of having her own baby.

Feeling her emotions bottle in her throat, she took a step back from Emily. "Four may be a little extreme, Luke. Probably a safe bet is between her second and third birthdays. You don't want to start her too soon. And put too much pressure on her. There are volumes of books written on the subject."

He let out a heavy sigh. "I'll never make it."

She reached out to pat his broad shoulder with reassurance, but then thought better of it. "Sure you will."

"How come you don't ever want to hold Emily?" Luke asked.

"W-what?" she stammered, her nerves twisting like ribbons and bows. "I-I don't know what you mean."

"You've never asked to hold her." Luke's gaze was curious but not condemning. "Every woman I've seen or met since Emily came into my life has wanted to hold her. She's practically snatched out of my arms in the grocery store. Why not you?"

"I-I…did. I put her in the crib earlier tonight."

"But you didn't hold her. There's a difference. You al-

most acted like she might be contagious. Trust me, you
can't get pregnant by holding a baby.''

She stiffened her spine and tried to keep her voice level.
''Trust me, I know the facts of life.'' And the cruelty.
''Look, Luke, I'm here to help you, not do the work for
you. Besides, it's important that Emily bond with her
daddy.''

She turned and headed out of the room, her legs feeling
unsteady, her heart unable to find a steady beat.

''Well, would you mind?'' He stopped her at the doorway.

Her pulse jumped sporadically. Afraid she knew exactly
what he meant, she asked, ''Mind what?''

She realized she *had* been avoiding the baby. It was for
self-preservation. She *needed* to avoid the baby.

''Hold her for a minute. I've got...'' he cleared his throat
''...an errand of my own. I'll just be a minute.''

''Oh'' was all she could manage. Squaring her shoulders,
she steeled her nerves and walked toward him, her legs
feeling stiff and unresponsive. ''Come here, Emily. Let's
let your daddy have a minute's worth of peace and quiet,
okay?''

Luke barely touched her as he set his little girl into her
arms. It was the exaggerated avoidance that Sydney noticed. It would have made her smile, if her disappointment
hadn't been so acute. Ridiculous, she thought. Why should
she want Luke to touch her? Already the sexual tension
had been too intense for her. Maybe it was like wiggling a
tooth, where one had to constantly keep pushing at the
loose molar for reassurance. Maybe it was the same with
Luke.

Her awareness of him irritated her, but it also made her
feel alive. It wasn't Luke, so much as the way a simple
brush of his hand gave her a warm tingle in the pit of her
stomach.

"Thanks." His gaze snagged hers.

Her breath caught. Her stomach dropped. It didn't take anything but a look from Luke to set her heart in motion. With her nerves a tangled mess, she jiggled the baby against her shoulder and purposefully shifted her attention away from Luke.

The baby's soft, pudgy arms wrapped around Sydney's neck. She breathed in the sweet scent of baby powder. Her apprehension dissipated with Emily's trusting smile. The pain Sydney had expected never materialized. Instead, a warmth filled an empty place in Sydney's heart. She enjoyed the softness of Emily's baby skin, heard that familiar crinkling of a diaper, felt the nourishing heat of a baby's body so close to hers. It brought back a flood of tender memories as she remembered rocking her little sister to sleep so long ago. It stirred up a torrent of emotions as she thought of the children she'd never give birth to, never rock to sleep, never watch grow.

All too quickly, yet not soon enough, Luke returned. "I appreciate your help," he said, taking Emily from her.

Her arms suddenly felt empty and a crack opened inside her heart. The pain of lost hopes and dreams seeped through her defenses. Snapping down on the pulsing ache, she shoved her despair into a dark corner of her heart and regained shaky control over her emotions. She wouldn't hold on to the past. No self-pity either. Instead, she'd look to her future. She had promise in her career. She'd nurture it and make it grow.

"Why don't you try rocking her back down?" she managed, her throat bunching. "She still looks pretty sleepy. I'll go check on the baklava." She needed a moment to herself, to push her longings back into the dark corner of her heart, to regain her shaky control over her emotions.

Luke nodded. "I won't be long. I hope."

Offering a halfhearted smile, she left the room, pausing

at the doorway for one last glimpse of him settling his large frame into the white rocker. Part of her wanted to offer to do this for him. She wanted...needed to hold Emily.

But she knew that would be a mistake. It was best if she stayed a distant observer instead of a participant. Hadn't Luke said he wanted to raise his daughter? That way, it would be easier for her to say goodbye after the baby shower. A longing squeezed her heart like Emily's little fist around her finger.

"Hey, there, Em, let's nod off to sleep now. Are you as tired as your daddy?" Luke started rocking back and forth, his voice lulling, soothing, comforting and somehow easing the ache in Sydney. "Maybe I don't make you play hard enough during the day, little one. Is that the problem? Is that why you like to keep your ol' pop up half the night? Maybe you need a playmate. Or a little brother or sister..."

Abruptly, Sydney turned away, not wanting to hear any more, wanting to keep her distance from Luke, his dreams, his plans, his hopes for a future family. A family, she reminded herself, that did not include her. Nor did she want it to.

A baby-fist grip tightened around her heart. No matter how wonderful Luke was, he was a man. Who wanted more children...his own children. And like Stan, her ex-husband, had said so often, "A man wants his own. Not a used car."

Fact was, she'd wanted her own, too. She'd wanted to feel a baby growing inside her, feel it kick and squirm. She'd wanted to hold her own baby, see the family resemblance in tiny hands, little feet, a button nose and blue eyes smiling back at her...her little piece of immortality. When she looked in the mirror, she saw her own mother staring back at her. Her mother might have died young but she'd left pieces of herself in each of her kids. When Sydney was gone, what piece of her would be left behind? Well-ordered accounting books?

Wrapping her arms across her middle, she entered the kitchen and fought her emotions back under control. No use crying over spilled milk. There wasn't anything she could do about her state of affairs. She couldn't have a baby. End of story.

But it wasn't. She still had a life. She'd make it fulfilling. Somehow. In the meantime, she'd remind herself that she wasn't burdened with the responsibility of raising a child. If she decided to move to Alaska, she could. And Luke wasn't the type of man she needed or wanted.

Sydney closed her eyes and inhaled deeply. "Mmm."

Luke caught himself staring at her upturned face, her parted lips. He'd followed her to the kitchen a few minutes after Emily had fallen back to sleep. Once again, his attention was immediately diverted to Sydney. He noticed the way her auburn hair curled around her shell-like ears, the twinkle in her blue eyes, the graceful way she moved her hands. When she drew in the buttery-sugar scent of the bubbling baklava, his gaze dropped to the soft curve of her breast. Damn! There he went again. Reacting to her. Wanting her.

Jerking his thoughts back to his task, he yanked open the oven and grabbed the pan. With a yelp, he jerked back. "Damn."

"What's wrong?" she asked, leaning close, close enough for him to suck in a whiff of wine, musky perfume and that elusive female scent that had desire curling in his belly like fingers into a tight fist.

"Nothing." He gritted his back teeth, having already forgotten about the burn on his hand. Frowning at his sophomoric libido, he grabbed a dish towel, then safely pulled the pan out of the oven and plunked it on the stove top.

She moved beside his left elbow, her hand reaching for his. Concern knitted her brow. "Are you okay?"

He pulled his hand out of her satiny grasp. "I'm fine."

This time, she grabbed his wrist with a firm grip and pried open his fingers to look at the red patch across his palm. "Sure you are. You just fried your hand."

He frowned but gave in like a recalcitrant child. Squirming as her gentle touch moved across his roughened, callused palm. He watched her delicate finger smooth over the pad of his thumb and around the sensitive edges of the burn. She tickled his nerve endings, and his fingers contracted. A mixture of pleasure and pain tormented him. The pleasure aroused him and became a rock hard pain in his gut.

"It's not blistering up," she said, her dainty features taut as she studied the angry welt. He wondered how long it had been since someone had worried about him. Too long. Even his mother had often been too absorbed with her own pain to fret over her only son. His heart contracted with the sight of Sydney's concern, with the tender touch of her hand, with her gentle insistence on helping him.

"Do you have any peas?"

He blinked. "Peas?"

"Frozen," she clarified. Pulling him along with her, she crossed the kitchen and opened the freezer door.

"What are you doing?" He sounded gruff as an old bear even to himself. He didn't want to be taken care of. It had always been his job to care for his mother, and now to care for Emily. He felt awkward, uncomfortable, like a child. Suddenly, her intense interest chafed him. "Are you suddenly hungry for a green vegetable?"

"Oh, corn, carrots, or even green beans will do."

She gave him a mysterious smile that tightened his nerves like a corkscrew as she settled a bag of frozen peas against his palm then closed his fingers over the cold plastic bag. "My mother used to do this when I burned myself. And her mother did it for her. So when I helped take care of my sister and brothers, I used this secret pea technique when they burned themselves. And now you can use it on Emily. Because all kids at one time or another get burned.''

He fisted the bag. "Feels weird."

So did her attention, her concern, her gentle caring.

"Wait till they defrost. I squished a lot of peas in my time. Emily will love it."

"I'm not letting Em in the kitchen," he stated, trying to ignore the chilling numbness along his palm.

"Then she'll be lucky." Her widening smile was contagious. He couldn't fight it. A grin spread across his face and somehow lightened the burden of his newfound responsibilities. Her smile vanished as quickly as it had appeared, leaving him confused. "But then Emily already is lucky." She wiped her hands on a paper towel. "She's got you for a dad.''

His thoughts tangled. Was he really a good father? After only a week? He had so much to learn. What if he made a mistake? What if he let Emily get hurt? What if he turned out to be like his own father? His doubts piled on top of each other until they seemed as imposing and unscalable as Mount Everest.

Turning, Sydney retreated to the baklava cooling on the stove. Her royal blue suit followed the curve of her figure, slanting from her shoulders to her narrow waist, then flaring at the hips. She'd discarded her pumps earlier and now stood in his kitchen in stocking feet. Her long legs, covered in creamy nylons, were as shapely as the rest of her and even more disconcerting to him.

"*Looks* edible," she said.

His throat closed. He licked his dry lips. *She certainly did.* Then he realized she was talking about the baklava. Focusing his gaze on the dessert, he felt his senses sharpening on her. "Did you have doubts?"

She placed a hand on his arm and set his nerve endings

on fire. "If you'd seen the batch I made, *you'd* have had doubts."

He chuckled and rubbed his thumb along his chin, carefully stepping away from her. "Looks healthy, don't you think?"

"You've got to be kidding. Didn't you see all the butter and sugar that went into these? And now we've got to pour some kind of sugary syrup all over it."

"It makes people feel good. So in my book, it's healthy." He drew in a deep breath of the buttery odor. "Soul food." He laughed at her startled look, and her cheeks reddened. "That's what my mother used to call chocolate chunk ice cream and pepperoni pizza. She used to say the more saturated fat, the more it comforted the hurting soul."

"Did she teach you how to cook?" She studied him.

"No. I think I learned in spite of her. Self-preservation. If I wanted something besides a box of macaroni and cheese or Hamburger Helper, then I had to fend for myself." He flung a dish towel over his right shoulder, as if cutting off the rest of that conversation. "Not bad," he said, analyzing the baklava, "for a first try."

"First try?" she repeated. "What do you mean?"

"We'll need to perfect our recipe. Play with it." He studied the diamond-cut pastries closer, avoiding Sydney's pursed lips that made him think of other games to be played.

"Haven't you made these before?" Her tone sounded stiff with sudden doubt.

"Uh." He realized his slip. He bent his head and examined the red, angry mark on his palm. Another dumb move. If he told her he only knew how to make chili, beer and now cinnamon apples thanks to his daughter, Sydney would be out the door faster than his own father.

And he didn't want her to leave. Not yet.

He needed more advice, more help with how to raise a daughter. But he knew it was more than that. And he didn't want it to be. Something about Sydney intrigued him. A woman who'd helped raise her siblings but couldn't cook worth a damn and rarely glanced at his daughter was far different from the women who'd oohed and aahed over Emily when he'd made mad dashes to the grocery store.

Then why didn't Sydney?

Maybe her lack of interest interested him.

Weirder things had happened.

It made no sense. What made even less was his blatant reaction to her like he was a sex-starved man. Until Emily had arrived, he'd had his share of recent dates. He wasn't counting, but he wasn't discounting them either. So with only a week of abstinence under his belt, so to speak, he was panting after some woman like a hormone-charged teenager.

"What I meant," he finally answered, "was that it was our first time together." He shook more cobwebs from his brain. That didn't sound right, either, dammit. "I mean, our first time to team-cook. That's not an easy task, you know?"

"You like to solo, then?" she asked, pink suffusing her cheeks as she ignored his blunder.

He shrugged.

She gave him a slow, easy smile. Her mouth tilted at the corner, a little lopsided. They'd both had too much wine. Maybe that explained his behavior, his sudden interest. But he knew he'd been interested since she'd first stepped into his house with her little bag of cookbooks. Long before wine had entered his system.

"So far," she said, "I think we make a pretty good team."

He swallowed. *Whoa, lady.*

His brain put on the brakes. His interest flew right out

the rear window. Hadn't all the women he'd ever dated
started with subtle hints like that? They always eased into
a discussion of the future, then they got irritated when he
stalled. They clung to him like vines, wanted and needed
more from him than he could give. He'd never promised
them anything. In fact, he'd always made it clear that he
wasn't marriage material. More than once, his date had
nodded her understanding, but the gleam in her eye had
meant she'd accepted his statement as a challenge.

But he'd decided long ago, back when he was a ten-
year-old boy, listening to his mother sobbing over his father's latest infidelity, that he wouldn't be like his dad. In
a way though, he worried that he was. How many women
had he dated? Too many to count. How many had he com-
mitted to?

The idea of a solid commitment always had him running
for the door. He squared his shoulders with determination.
Now, he had a reason to commit. But only to his baby. He
wouldn't back away or disappoint his daughter.

The thought of Emily tugged at his heart. He was stuck
now. Part of him felt trapped. Part of him felt damn for-
tunate. If Emily's mom hadn't given her up, he might have
never known that he had a daughter. He might have missed
her sweet smile, her soft hugs, her slobbery kisses that
made his heart contract. But which part of him would win
this inner struggle?

He wasn't sure. But he knew for certain that he didn't
have anything to offer women...or Sydney. Not now.
Maybe not ever.

Wait a minute. He'd put the dessert before the entrée.
He wasn't dating Sydney. She seemed as gun-shy as he
was about relationships and marriage. So what was he worried about? Why was he retreating at the mere thought of
working as a team with this woman? Was he fighting her
or his own desires?

Again, she breathed in the scent of the flaky pastries, arching her back and emphasizing her pert, round breasts, perfect for the size of a man's hands. He knew then, *he* was the reason he should worry.

"Smells yummy," she said. "Like a slice of heaven. What was that last spice you added?"

"Cloves," he answered automatically, unable to focus on anything but the idea of kissing her. Where had that come from? Why was he torturing himself like this? Reminding himself they weren't compatible, that she was career-oriented and he was a single father with responsibilities, he shook off those steamy thoughts.

"Hmm. Maybe that was the added spice my boss couldn't remember." She licked her bottom lip, and his gaze followed the moist trail she left along the pink swell. His stomach knotted. His mind shut down completely. "It gives it some zest. The ones I made...well, they didn't look this...this appetizing. And the one I sampled..." She squinched up her face, like Emily when she tried one of his homemade concoctions, right before she spewed it out "...it tasted like soggy cereal. No zip."

"You mean, no snap, crackle and pop?"

She stared at him. Then she laughed, the robust sound bursting out of her, tumbling over him. It wasn't a twitter, a giggle or a simper. It was a full-bodied laugh that shook her shoulders, crinkled her eyes and captivated him. Okay, his joke wasn't *that* funny, but he liked a woman who could laugh, really laugh. At herself, at life. His mother hadn't been able to do that. She'd wallowed in self-pity. And Sheila hadn't laughed at life, herself or him. But she was probably laughing now, as she got a full night's sleep and no longer worried about diaper changes or early-morning feedings.

Was Sydney that much different? Not from her linen suits and medium-sized pumps, pearls and polished look.

She'd said she'd already raised three kids that weren't her own. She didn't want to raise Emily, too. But something about her made him feel entirely different.

And that made him nervous.

He escaped to the other side of the kitchen, yanking open the refrigerator and letting the chilled air sift over him. He needed a beer. No, he didn't. Maybe coffee would be a better bet. "We'd best make that syrup."

She nodded and started organizing the material she'd brought. He started the coffee percolating and mixed the sugar and water for the syrup in a saucepan. She added the honey and stopped when he said, "Whoa." When the mixture looked like fine spun gold, he poured it over the top of the pastry.

Twirling his spatula like a gunfighter's six-shooter, he said, "Let's give it a try."

"But I thought it had to rest for twenty-four hours."

"Huh?" he asked, skimming through recipes in his mind.

"It needs time to soak up the syrup and...I don't know what else. That's just what I read."

His brow furrowed as he stared at the sugary concoction. "Looks good though. I guess we could wait till tomorrow." Suddenly, he grinned at her. "Or we could sample it now and then again tomorrow."

She laughed at his eager expression. "All right. You talked me into it."

He served her a diamond wedge of the ooey-gooey pastry, dripping with butter and thick golden syrup. The walnuts glistened like amber nuggets along the layers.

Blowing gently on the pastry, she pursed her lips and bit into it. A tiny crumb affixed to the edge of her bottom lip. He resisted catching it. He ignored it. Or tried to. He yanked his gaze away from staring at her mouth. But that damn flake drew his gaze straight back to her full, pouty lip.

Confused, not sure what to do, feeling guilty for not telling her about the crumb on her lip, he rubbed his jaw and glanced down at the floor, hoping it would be gone. When he shifted his gaze back to her, hoping for a response of some kind for the baklava, the tiny flake was still on the edge of her lip. Focusing on her expression that flickered and changed, he felt the tension inside him coil like a red-hot grill. "Well…"

Thankfully, she rolled her lips together and snagged the crumb with her tongue. Drawing a deeper breath, he waited, impatient for her reaction.

Slowly, she nodded and swallowed. "It's good."

Disappointment doused his expectations. Good. Not great. Not even a "mmm…good." Damn.

He popped one of the pastries in his mouth, chewed, deciphered the seasonings and dissected the texture. "Not bad," he surmised, more aware of Sydney than the warm pastry in his mouth. "Not what I'd hoped for, but we can work from here. Maybe by tomorrow, the flavors will have blended."

"This isn't what you wanted?"

"Nope."

"What's it supposed to taste like?" she asked, sampling more of hers in tiny nibbles.

"You mean you don't know?"

She shook her head. "Not really."

An idea flickered in his head, caught and held a distinct flame. What could it hurt? After all, he'd been stuck at home with a baby, and no one to really talk to, no adult conversation, no real food other than his attempts at the baby food market. "Then we've got to take a field trip."

"Huh?" Sydney's blue eyes widened, reminding him of

the Caribbean's vivid color. "What do you mean?" He liked the way her eyes tipped up at the corners. "A date?"

"No." His denial came too abruptly.

Sydney actually looked relieved. The crinkle in her brow disappeared, the worry darkening her gaze lifted. He stuck to his answer like glue. She'd already made it clear this was strictly business. But other ideas teased his mind, dangerous as they might be. On the other hand, maybe she'd be a safe date. She didn't seem interested in a single father with a kid.

She had her plans. He had his.

She was an accountant. He'd be helping Emily count to ten, name colors, cut and paste.

He almost laughed at himself for thinking of Sydney, with her shapely figure and expressive mouth, as safe. Safe from him? He doubted it.

"A field trip," he reemphasized.

Suddenly, she gave him a tilted smile that clouded his brain once more. He figured she'd regret her decision in the morning. "Okay. A field trip. For baklava."

"And soufflés," he added. It might take several trips to cover the different types of desserts she'd planned for the baby shower. Strange, how that didn't make him nervous.

"Don't forget the crème brûlée."

He nodded. But what about Emily? He couldn't leave her home. Alone. Disappointment sifted through him, followed by a good helping of guilt. He *was* like his father. Ready to run. His roving eye always trained on a pretty woman. Well, dammit, he wouldn't be like that. Not now. Not with Emily.

It wasn't practical to never look at another woman or even forsake going on dates. But he should stay as far away as possible from anything that might distract him from his number one obligation—Emily. A woman like Sydney, who attracted him like a starving man to a backyard bar-

becue, definitely distracted him. She was almost too delicious for him to find the willpower to resist.

"It won't work. I can't go," he said, his determination
solid. "Who would take care of Emily?"

Stunned by his sudden change, Sydney stared at him. She
wasn't letting him out of it that easily. Maybe he'd had a
change of heart. Maybe he'd instantly regretted asking her
out. But she needed this…field trip. Nervous at the pros-
pect, she preferred the idea of an outing for research pur-
poses. He'd been right. She needed to know what the desserts should taste like.

"Get a baby-sitter," she answered, shrugging off his
concern.

"I'm not leaving my child with a stranger."

"It doesn't have to be a stranger," she said, her determination growing.

Sure, she thought, she could go by herself. But Luke
understood the culinary arts much better than she. He
would know the best places to go. For some insane reason,
she trusted him.

And she didn't want to go alone.

After a year of being on her own, she'd learned to do
almost everything with only herself as company. She
shopped, ate, studied, slept by herself. All alone. At night,
when she curled beneath the comforter, loneliness crept into
her apartment.

She didn't want to do this by herself, too.

Worse, she wanted Luke to be the one with her. Which
seemed dangerous to her equilibrium. This man, with his
dark, wavy hair and intense eyes and sun-brightened smile,
tilted her world. More than anything, she needed to feel
centered.

But his charm didn't distract her from her more important goal.

"It could be a neighbor. A friend. A relative," she named the possibilities. "My little sister could do it." At his dubious glance, she added. "She's twenty and attending college here in Dallas. She's very good with kids. She's going to be a teacher."

"What if something were to happen? I'd never forgive myself." He shook his head and stuffed his hands in his jean pockets. "No, I better stay here with Emily."

"So, because you have a baby now, you're going to give up your entire life. Your career. Your social life."

"I told you," he said, grinding his teeth, "I don't believe in turning my kid over to a day care, a nanny, or anybody. Emily is my responsibility. Mine. Nobody else's.

"Her own mother didn't want her. What if I were to walk out on her, too? How would that affect her? Would I be showing her that no one cares enough to sacrifice anything for her? Until she's older, until she can understand, I'm staying."

His words pulled the breath right out of Sydney. She stared at Luke for several erratic heartbeats. Unnerved by his devotion, moved by his sincerity, touched by his commitment, she remembered her ex-husband, his easy disregard of her feelings, his dismissal of their vows, his contempt for their love and promises to cleave to one another during good and bad times. The first major rock in the road and he'd turned around and plunged into another woman's arms...a woman who was fertile...a "real woman."

She remembered his words when he'd told her he was leaving Sydney for his girlfriend. "Hell," Stan had said with a hiss, "Lucy's pregnant. With my kid. I can't turn my back on her. She needs me." Later, he confided in Sydney, "Lucy's a real woman." And he'd turned his back on Sydney when she'd most needed his understanding, his love. But she'd discovered he'd never truly loved her. He sure hadn't loved her once he'd learned she was infertile.

The ache behind her eyes and burning tears resurfaced. Over and over, he'd told her she was worthless, useless. And she'd believed him. But not anymore. She was doing something with her life. She was accomplishing things.

In awe, she watched this man across from her. Luke had responded to the surprise arrival of his daughter with honor. This man, this caring father, loved his daughter more than anything. At that moment, he was the most attractive man she'd ever met.

"Since it's just a field trip," she said, her heart beating its way into her throat, "then it's okay if she goes with us."

Emily would be their chaperone. She'd dull the attraction between Sydney and Luke. The baby would constantly remind Sydney there was no future with Luke, even when she was tempted by him.

"A ten-month-old at a fancy restaurant?" he asked. "This should be interesting."

Chapter Four

The coffeehouse was noisy but filled with a kinetic energy.

Sydney felt the dynamic beat in her chest. She didn't know if it was from the guitar music pulsing through the restaurant, the exuberant laughter from the customers at the tables nearby, or if it was the easy way Luke smiled at her.

That made her feel anything but relaxed.

His dark eyes radiated a softer light when he looked from his daughter to her, reminding her of melting chocolate. A rippling awareness undulated through her.

Luke shouldn't affect her this way.

She wouldn't allow it.

Because *this,* she reminded herself, was not a date. It wasn't even a date night. It was a plain old, boring Tuesday. The other customers crowding the coffeehouse were still wearing their work clothes—uniforms, loosened ties with corporate suits and crinkled linen dresses, like her own.

This…this outing was a field trip. Nothing else.

Inside her churning mind, she discovered the simple reason behind the sudden wash of awareness for Luke—it had been too long since she'd been out on the town. A sense of relief loosened the tightness along her shoulders.

"One order of baklava and the mocha soufflé," Luke stated, "plus two cups of coffee." His gaze shifted from the waitress to his daughter strapped in the high chair beside him. "Better bring her…" Confusion crinkling his brow, he glanced at Sydney. "What can she eat?"

His question startled her out of her thoughts and gave her something concrete to consider. She folded the plastic-covered menu and handed it to the waitress. "Do you have vanilla ice cream?"

"Orange sherbet, I believe." The young woman smiled and stuck her ordering pad in her back jeans pocket. She couldn't have been older than Jennie, Sydney's own little sister.

It gave Sydney a stitch of misgivings over the argument she'd had with Jennie the day before. As the roles they'd always maintained started to change, their relationship was suffering growing pains.

"We'll have a cup then for the baby," Luke told the waitress.

She nodded. "I'll have your order right out."

An awkward silence settled upon their table. Luke shifted in his seat, crossing one ankle over the other knee. His foot brushed her skirt, and Sydney practically jumped out of her skin. All of her sensors went on full alert. She scooted her chair back a measly fraction and smoothed a hand down her skirt, molding the fabric along the front of her shin. The scant distance between them wasn't enough to settle her nerves. The laughter and lively discussion around their too-small table exaggerated the lull in conversation with Luke. Sydney wasn't sure if she wanted to fill the space with idle chatter or let the pause lengthen and grow, increasing the space between them.

She caught Luke staring at her from across the table, his eyes hooded, his mouth quirked in a sexy knee-weakening half smile. Something about him, maybe his vulnerability with Emily, his desperate need for help or his reckless confidence in the kitchen made her want to know more about him. Her pulse skittered. Nervous, she looked away and made a production out of unwrapping her silverware and placing the linen napkin in her lap. For some reason, he made her jittery, as if she was about to face the IRS.

Emily began fussing and distracted Sydney from the baby's father. Grunting with frustration, the baby shifted and pushed against the metal tray on the high chair. She stuck her hand in her mouth, gnawing on her fist until drool covered the chubby little hand. Her tiny brow wrinkled, and Sydney knew a crying fit was about to erupt.

"Did you bring her lamb?" she asked, hoping to entertain the baby with a familiar toy.

"We brought everything, including the kitchen sink." Luke chuckled. The warm, husky sound rolled over her like a summer heat wave. Confidently, he reached for the pink tote that Emily's mom had handed over along with the baby almost two weeks ago.

She watched his large hands rummage through the frilly pink-and-white lace diaper bag. It brought a smile to Sydney's heart.

"Diapers. Bottle. Sanitary wipes." He laid the items on the table and kept digging.

Emily became more agitated. She fought against the safety strap around her waist. Sydney had no doubts that when the baby decided to scream her frustration, she'd make more noise than the laughter, lilting guitar music and clinking dishes combined. A couple at the next table paused in their conversation to stare at baby Emily.

"Desitin. Ambusol. Changing blanket," Luke continued, naming all the items Sydney had recommended he bring.

"Pacifier. Cloth diaper. Change of clothes." He glanced up with a panicked expression, his hand patting the inside of the bag, the table littered with small piles of baby paraphernalia. "No lamb," he said, his voice tight. "What do we do?"

Sydney poked through the soft, pink blanket and pushed the medicine out of Emily's reach. "We can always—"

"Here! This will work." Luke stuck a spoon in his daughter's hand. "Emily, play with this."

Immediately, the baby's eyes widened with surprise. Her mouth opened wide with a suddenly happy smile. She gummed the smooth, round metal. Emitting a gleeful sound, she twisted her wrist and waved the spoon in the air as if it were a trophy.

"That worked like a charm." Luke sat back, his shoulders relaxing, a smile brightening his rugged features, as if he'd just won father of the year.

"Um," Sydney said, hating to take away his proud smile, "that's probably not a—"

Clank! Emily banged the spoon against the metal tray. *Clank! Clank!*

Several heads turned toward them. Laughing a gurgling sound, Emily clacked the spoon down again and again, beating the tray. The noise sent a bolt of electricity up Sydney's spine. Her eardrums vibrated with the noise.

Shaking her head, she said, "Not a good idea."

A frown settled between Luke's brows. "Now what?" he called across the table over the crescendoing noise. Surrounding conversations sputtered to a stop. The guitar player strummed harder, making the strings squeal, as he tried to drown out Emily's drum playing. Those beside them glared their irritation.

"Do I take it away?" Luke asked. "Will that make her mad? What then?"

Tempted to cover her own ears, Sydney managed, "Not

if you replace it with something else. Just put the spoon out of sight.''

With her encouraging nod, Luke wrestled the spoon out of Emily's slippery grasp. Sydney reached for the pacifier at the same time Luke did. His hand covered hers briefly. Their gazes locked. Heat shimmied through her. She froze. Slowly, he removed his hand from hers. But his intense gaze remained steady, acute. He jumbled her nerves, like one of her disorganized client's accounting books. Her hand trembled as she clutched the pacifier. As if it was burning a hole in her hand, she jabbed it into the baby's mouth and returned her hand to her lap—where it belonged.

An appreciative silence swelled in the restaurant before the other customers turned back toward their tables. Quiet conversations began again. The musician picked up in the middle of ''You are My Sunshine.'' And Sydney turned a deaf ear to Luke's rendition as he tried to gain his daughter's attention.

''You're good,'' he said, his voice low, warm and inviting. Admiration shone in his dark eyes. She caught him watching her, his eyes dark and mysterious.

''I'm experienced. That's all.'' With a shaky smile, she lifted the bib off the table. She had to get out more often, she decided. Maybe then Luke wouldn't...bother her. ''And soon you'll be experienced, too.''

Luke started cramming all the baby items back into the diaper bag in a haphazard manner. It didn't fit as nicely this time, and he had to push down on a couple of diapers. ''I don't know if I'll ever remember everything.''

''Sure you will. Trial and error. That's how you learn to be a parent.'' Memories shifted through her mind like old photographs, replaying tantrums, arguments, standoffs. With each one, Sydney had learned. She hoped her siblings hadn't suffered too much at her inabilities.

She held out the bib for him, letting it dangle by a plastic strip between her two fingers as if it—or Luke—had cooties. He took it from her, carefully avoiding touching her again. Still, his look made her insides itch. Straightening her spine, she sat back in her chair and resisted the weird effect he had on her.

"You can be given some parental advice, but until you experience things firsthand…" She paused, trying to think of the right example. "Like I could tell you never to ask Emily, when she's two, if she wants to take a bath or not. You never give a two-year-old a choice, unless you're willing to accept no as her answer. Instead, you give them choices, like which towels do they want to use. Or which bubble bath.

"But until you make that fatal error yourself, until your kid defiantly says no, until you try cramming a screaming child into a bathtub, you don't really learn that valuable lesson."

Luke rubbed his jaw thoughtfully. "Sounds like an experience you won't forget."

She grinned. Yes, she'd made mistakes, but she'd learned from them. And she didn't mind sharing her knowledge with this eager father. In fact, she realized at that moment, she rather liked it. "I didn't make that mistake twice. My sister could wail and carry on with the best of them. So, I learned quickly."

"You should have your own kids." He zipped the diaper bag with a decisive movement and at the same time unraveled her composure.

You should have your own kids.

How many times had she wished for that very blessing? Grateful to be sitting, Sydney thought she might have fallen onto the floor otherwise, her knees buckling beneath the weight of her despair. A chill settled over her entire body. Her insides started to quake with the effort to maintain her emotions. As if she were in a vacuum, she heard Emily's contended sucking sounds on the pacifier. She wished for peace and contentment. But she didn't think she'd ever find it. Instead, she'd pushed her restless energy toward a full-time career. Which was why she was here in the first place. Where was that baklava?

Across the table, she felt Luke's gaze piercing through the walls she'd built around her heart until he found her most vulnerable spot. Could he see her pain? Could he see her longings?

She wondered what it would be like to watch her own child, a baby that had grown inside her, laughing and playing. What would it feel like to hold that creation in her arms, rock her baby to sleep, tell her child that she loved it more than anything? The heat of regret and disappointment burned her throat.

"But I guess," he fumbled, "like you said, you've already raised your kids...your brothers and sister." Full of interest, he looked squarely into her eyes. "Did you always want to be an accountant?"

"No." She barely managed to force the word through her tight throat. Her heart yearned for her own child, longed to experience the wonder and joy Luke had been blessed with. Instead, her heart ached with a bitter emptiness.

She gave a hearty dose of reality to her poisonous thoughts. She'd reconciled herself to the facts. As an accountant, she relied on numbers and percentages. They never lied or deceived. They never let her down. Not like life. She'd faced facts. And she'd gotten on with her life. How, then, had this man and his baby uncovered her secret yearnings?

Emily's pacifier clunked onto the metal tray. Luke slipped it back between her lips. Watching his large hand holding that soft pink plastic, Sydney felt a tightness seize her chest.

"I guess some women," he said, his tone implying he

meant her, "want their careers more than home and family." She didn't detect a chauvinistic attitude, only a simple statement of fact.

Her throat burned. She wanted to tell him she'd had no choice. She wanted to stomp her feet and bang on something as Emily had. Instead, she gave a weak smile to the waitress who set two cups of coffee on their table. The baby lunged for the steaming cups, and Sydney easily moved them out of Emily's reach.

Her hand trembled as she poured a dollop of cream in the black liquid. Gripping the spoon as she held onto her dignity, she stirred in a generous portion of sugar. The cream and sugar combined and turned the dark brew a lighter shade, much as her dreams and longings had been forced to change over the years. "Some women can manage both," she stated, her voice sturdier than she felt. "Families and careers. Some can't."

Luke sampled his straight black coffee, sucking in the steaming brew with a grimace. Sydney's words were true and struck him with the force of a sharp jab. His shoulders tightened. His jaw clenched. Feeling old anxieties and shame twist his insides, he admitted, "My mom couldn't."

Sydney frowned, her smooth brow puckering with curiosity. "What do you mean?"

Luke twined the plastic strands of Emily's bib around his index finger, feeling the tightness inside him grow taut with old memories. He'd never sat in judgment of his mother. He'd loved her as any son would. He'd wanted to protect her with the fierceness of a lion. He held no blame, no remorse in his heart for the things he'd forfeited in order to help her. But he'd begun to realize as he took care of Emily, as he watched and listened to Sydney, what he'd missed as a child.

"She never wanted to do anything but stay home and

raise kids,'' he said, his throat tense. "But when my dad left, she...fell apart.''

He remembered his mom's inconsolable tears, her fear, his own helplessness. She'd been heartsick over his father leaving her for another woman. She'd been terrified of finding a job, convinced she couldn't do anything besides cook and clean. As a little boy, he'd cried with his mom, cursed his dad, and stuffed his fears deep inside him. He'd had to be strong. He'd had to grow up quickly.

"You were an only child then?'' Sydney asked, her voice soft and comforting.

He nodded. "I was seven when they divorced.''

In his heart, he could still hear his mom crying, her sobs muffled by a pillow and the closed bedroom door separating them. Some days she'd never changed out of her bathrobe. Most days, she'd moped around the house, munching on junk food, watching old reruns on the television.

"That must have been so hard. On her.'' Her voice grew husky with emotion, not pity but understanding, and Luke's attention shifted back to Sydney. "And you.''

He shrugged, feeling uncomfortable with her sympathy, with her undivided attention. He'd gotten over it a long time ago. He'd put it behind him, as he had his relationship with his father. He wondered if Sydney had gotten past her divorce. Had she reacted as his mother had? Had she suffered the same despair? Had she been paralyzed with grief and fear?

"How did your mom take care of you?'' she asked, lifting the mug to her lips.

"I took care of her.''

As if he were catapulted back in time, he could smell the sweet earthy scent of peanut-butter-and-jelly sandwiches—his after-school specialty. He'd take a sandwich and big glass of milk to his mother and crawl into bed with her. She'd turn off the sound on some soap opera, munch politely on his sandwich and ask him questions about his day. But she hadn't really listened, not the way Sydney was listening to him now.

"Sounds like you helped raise your mom, the way I helped raise my brothers and sister." Sydney's comment held no recriminations, only deep understanding for a difficult situation. She punctuated her statement by reaching across the table and placing a hand on his arm, surprising him with her warmth, her compassion and his own foolish response.

The heat of her seeped through the sleeve of his jersey. The cold icy shell he'd placed around his heart so long ago began to melt. He tensed, uncomfortable with the connection being forged between them.

"Was your mom like that for long?" she asked, searching for honesty when other women had wanted to avoid such a painful topic. Touched by this woman, he felt a friendship form. One he hadn't anticipated. Or wanted. But it was there. As if their childhoods, hurting, aching, needing, similar yet so different, had somehow bonded them in the present in a comforting but at the same time unnerving way.

"A while," he said, unwilling to delve too much into his own painful past.

His father had shattered his mother's confidence, her sense of security, her dreams of the future. Luke remembered helping his mom fill out her first job application for a restaurant near their house. When she'd landed the waitressing job, they'd celebrated with glasses of milk and chocolate chip cookies. That had been the first time he'd seen his mother smile in months. It had warmed him all the way down to his tennis shoes. After that monumental achievement, Luke had met his mother at her work every afternoon when school let out. He'd hung out in the kitchen, waiting for her to finish her shift. It had been his first experience with the restaurant business. The memories still brought a warm smile to his lips.

As he thought of the role reversal between his mother and him, he wondered if he'd rebelled against being the nurturer, the strong one, and had in essence turned into his own father. Maybe that's why he'd avoided commitments in his past relationships.

He felt Sydney's gaze on him, warm and steady. Her thumb brushed across his knuckles and her fingers curled around his hand. She was soft and stirred something inside him that he'd never been aware of before. Somehow, she made him want to open his heart. But he resisted.

"My dad," she said, "was devastated by my mom's death. Home reminded him of her loss. So, he buried himself in his work and relied on me to take care of the other kids. Your mom and my dad suffered different blows, but the results were the same."

Looking into her deep blue eyes full of compassion and strength, he knew she understood what he'd felt as a child. "Lots of responsibility."

He wondered if it had been too much for Sydney's fragile shoulders at times. Had she buckled as his mother had? He doubted that. Sydney was resourceful, resilient. She had confidence, a sense of purpose. As he had. Their own inner strengths had sustained them through their own ordeals.

He caught sight of the waitress approaching, and their conversation ended as quickly as it had begun. Sydney sat back, pulling her hand away from his. He instantly missed the contact. His heart felt deprived of the brief connection they'd made. Irritated at his foolishness, he pushed his coffee to the side as the waitress set the plate of baklava in front of him.

"Looks good," he replied, a jaunty smile replacing the seriousness of the moment before.

"Nothing like the batch I fixed at home," Sydney said, laughter making her voice lilt affectionately.

Emily lunged for her bowl of orange sherbet, launching herself across the metal tray separating her from the small round table. With quick reflexes, Luke moved the bowl out of her reach. Tapping his daughter playfully on the nose, he smiled. "Not yet, sugar. Let's put your bib on first. Don't want ice cream all over your pretty pink dress."

Emily studied him with somber, dark eyes. Her chubby hand opened and shut as she continued reaching for the sherbet. Little grunts of exasperation escaped her parted, bow-like lips.

Sydney chuckled. "She probably doesn't care. In a few minutes, we'll all be wearing it anyway."

"Not if I can help it." He hooked the bib Sydney had suggested he bring around Emily's little neck. His fingers fumbled with the plastic ties. He cursed softly under his breath before he managed to tie the strings.

Settling back into his own seat, he dipped a spoon into the soft sherbet. Emily leaned forward, her mouth open, eager for the bite. The cold made her blink, then she pushed it out with her tongue and the orange glob rolled down and plopped in her lap. She dipped her chin and shook her head back and forth.

Luke frowned. "She hates it."

"Give her a chance. She may not have had ice cream before."

Luke tried another spoonful, this time a small sampling. The sherbet melted on the baby's tongue, and she offered them a syrupy smile.

Laughing, he said, "You do like it. Here's some more, Em."

When he pushed another spoonful toward his daughter, Emily grabbed the spoon. It didn't take long before orange goop was sliding down the length of her arm and residing in her hair.

"Emily!" He grabbed a napkin. Soon, orange sherbet dotted his jersey, and Emily smeared a glob across the metal tray.

"She's okay," Sydney said. "Let her play. We'll clean up the mess before we leave."

His frown deepened for a moment as he watched his daughter finger paint with the sticky goop. Slowly, he relaxed, feeling his features soften. A smile tugged at his mouth. Awed by the wonder of his child, he felt a chuckle rumble in his chest.

"You know," Luke said, "I never thought I'd enjoy having a child. But now, I can't imagine not having Emily. Playing with her makes me wonder if my parents ever really enjoyed me. Or if I was a reminder of an unhappy marriage."

"Oh, Luke. I'm sure they loved you like you love Emily."

He remained silent a moment, doubting her comment. Finally, he said, his voice thick, "It's a shame every child can't remember times like this with one's folks."

"Maybe we do. Maybe it's just subconscious."

His throat contracted with deep emotions he'd never contacted before. "I hope I never lose this."

Moisture swelled in Sydney's blue eyes. "Cherish each moment." Her voice wavered. "They grow up so fast."

"Did you have time to do that?" He wondered what her life had been like as a child, trying to grow up while raising her brothers and sister. How had she managed? How had she coped?

She stared down at her ringless left hand, silent, contemplative. He sensed he'd somehow crossed an invisible line.

"Didn't mean to pry. It's none of my business."

She shook her head, and the light from overhead played

in the strands of her red hair. "It's okay." But her voice sounded rough, as if it raked over her emotions before the words came out of her mouth. "I'm okay. Just sentimental." She sniffed daintily. "Sometimes I miss those busy, frantic days when I had to study for a social studies test, make the beds, pack lunches for all of us, be sure Jennie, Paul and Scott had done their homework and somehow manage to do my own."

A wisp of a smile touched her lips and his heart. "Didn't leave a lot of time for yourself...or dating."

She shrugged, the same noncommittal, inconsequential shrug he'd used earlier. Was it to hide an overwhelming sense of pain and loss, too? "It wasn't important until I went to college."

"So you got away finally?"

"My dad insisted. But I wouldn't leave home, so we compromised on a local school in Tulsa. That's where I met Stan. And all my troubles began." A note of laughter tried to lift her words but the smile never reached her eyes.

Suddenly he wanted to know more about her marriage, her divorce, her heartache. She'd loved a man. For some insane reason, Luke felt a tightness in his abdomen, a fire in his belly. He tried to focus on the fact that he'd never fallen in love. Maybe this was simple curiosity. Maybe he wanted a reminder of what could happen if he released his heart. Maybe he needed that reminder now, more than ever, as he grew closer to and more interested in Sydney.

"Your husband?" he prompted.

"My ex."

"How long have you been divorced?"

"A year." She rolled her fork over, the tablecloth muting the sound.

"How long had you been married?" He couldn't stop the questions from firing out of his mouth.

"Over five years." Her voice sounded strained. She took a sip of coffee, and he noticed her hand shook.

He spooned more sherbet into Emily's open mouth. Most of it ended up in the orange swirls on the metal tray or staining her mouth. She swallowed and gurgled with satisfaction. Enthusiastically, she clapped her hands, asking for more. Slowly, Luke's gaze shifted back to Sydney.

"What was he like?" Luke asked, more curious about her reasons for marrying than he should have been.

"Stan?" She paused as if gathering her thoughts. She shoved her fingers through her short hair and shifted in her seat. He wondered if his question had made her nervous or angry. "Stanley Elliott Wagner." She sighed heavily as if her ex-husband was a burden to even think about. "We met in college. He was a couple of years older than me. I was a young college freshman, only seventeen, and pretty naive. But in many ways I felt far older than most of my friends."

He nodded, impressed by her devotion to her family. He understood it, because he'd felt the same things for his mother.

She studied her coffee cup, running her finger around the rim, then glanced at Emily. But she avoided returning Luke's gaze. "When he graduated, I was afraid he'd leave school and forget about me. So I agreed to marry him."

She shook her head. "I know, dumb move. But I was young...naive...and stupid."

Luke watched her closely. Watched how her fingers curled into her palms, her short nails digging perfect little moon shapes into her flesh. She had delicate hands. But they were usually steady. Her jaw often jutted forward with confidence and determination. Her cool veneer seemed to crumble before his eyes. Her shoulders hunched forward. Her chin dipped low. She stared down at the table, trying to shade her emotions from him.

He noted that she hadn't claimed to be so in love with her husband that she'd given up her chance for her education. Had she never loved Stan? Or had the divorce killed even the memory of those tender feelings?

"Anyway—" she let out a breath "—we married. I had to quit school for a while. I worked and helped pay his tuition. Later, after he'd graduated, then I went to school at night, after I'd worked all day. It took me even longer, but I finally managed to get my degree. Strange how a diploma doesn't mean you've learned everything you need to know."

Luke felt his eyebrows arching with silent questions.

"I guess my late-night study habits took a toll on my marriage. Or maybe I wasn't around enough." She shrugged and let the silence envelop their table.

"Don't say you didn't cook or clean well enough for Stan."

A chuckle escaped her tense lips. "I probably didn't do that enough either. I think I was tired of cooking and cleaning after so many years of taking care of my siblings. Or maybe I figured he was old enough to feed himself. Anyway, about the time I got my diploma, Stan had gotten himself another woman."

An expletive shot out of Luke's mouth before he could catch it. His gaze immediately shifted to Emily. He drew a relieved breath when he realized his daughter wasn't paying attention to anything but her sticky fingers.

Sydney's mouth puckered in a frown. He could see the devastation in the midnight depths of her eyes.

"Of course, I didn't know right away. My salary helped furnish a nice home for them. I didn't realize he was buying her so many things on his credit card. Finally, Stan had to confess. I packed my bags and moved to Dallas."

"Where had you been living?"

"Kansas City."

"Why Dallas?" His curiosity about Sydney multiplied by the minute and his admiration for her spirit soared.

She shook her head. "My sister was going to school down here. And my brothers were living in the area. So in a way, it was like coming home."

Something glimmered in her eyes. Pain. He would have recognized it anywhere. He saw the tiny muscles in her hands tighten. He waited for her to go on. For her to tell him more. But she grew silent.

Then he saw a single tear slip down her soft, pale cheek. His abs clenched tight as if he'd been hit. He leaned forward and wiped it away, the moisture burning into his skin. "Syd...Sydney, I'm sorry. I shouldn't have—"

"It's not your fault." She tried a shaky smile.

He edged his chair closer and felt her silk-covered calf brush his leg. Distracted, he felt his mouth go dry.

With every ounce of determination, he forced himself to meet her gaze, forced himself to concentrate on her pain. Raw emotion swirled in those blue depths and absorbed him immediately.

"Are you still in love with him...your ex?" he gently probed, surprised at the tension building inside him as he waited, too aware he'd be disappointed if she said yes.

"No. Definitely not." Honesty and surety rang in her voice. Relief filtered through him. Her hand seemed to steady at that moment, as if she had no doubts about her ex. "His infidelity cured me of any feelings I had. Now, I feel nothing."

She looked pale, and he cursed himself. He wished he could take away her pain. She looked at him with oceans of blue in her eyes. He could have drowned in the swirling depths. He responded to her like the ocean reacts to the moon.

"What hurt the most..." She paused, twisting her fingers together. Her bottom lip trembled. She bit down on it, turning the pink skin white. "Stan got *her*...that woman pregnant."

Anger shot through him.

Her hand clenched into a fist. He sensed it wasn't anger she battled. He deciphered her reaction and realized she fought to control her emotions that churned and swelled in the depths of her eyes. He read self-pity and a deep, heartbreaking sadness.

Anger burned inside him. It was the same feeling he'd had as a child for his mother, when his own father had walked out of their lives for a younger woman.

"I felt sorry for myself for a while." She lifted her shoulders into a straight line. His admiration for her grew. She was a survivor. "I'm okay now."

But was she? She didn't look as confident as her words sounded. She looked a little lost, a lot rejected.

Suddenly, she shot out of her chair and headed toward the door. He blinked, stunned at her departure. Guilt wrenched his gut. He'd asked too many damn questions. He'd stabbed at her long-buried pain. And he raced after her.

When he caught her with a hand on her elbow, he turned her to face him. Her tears scalded his heart. Pressing his hand against her cheek, he cupped her jaw, curled his fingers along the fine bone and satiny smooth skin. He felt her lean into him. As if she needed him. He relished the heady feeling. His body vibrated and hummed. He wanted to give her back her smile.

In Sydney, he detected an underlying strength. Her courage drew him like a powerful magnet. He hadn't been able to help his mother. But dammit, he could help Sydney. He could show her, prove to her, she was a sexy woman, deserving of being cherished.

She looked at him with those fathomless, watery blue eyes, and he couldn't resist the potent attraction. He bent his head down. Her eyes widened. Her lips parted, with invitation or surprise, he wasn't sure. So, he kissed her.

Her mouth was softer than he'd expected, sweeter. The taste of cream and sugar lingered on her lips along with the subtle flavor of hazelnut. Her softness challenged the hard callous side of him, rubbing against him like velvet, unnerving him.

A crash behind him shattered the surreal moment, their kiss.

Dammit! Panic arced through him. He'd forgotten Emily.

Chapter Five

Before Luke turned away from Sydney, away from her glistening mouth and startled blue eyes and the intimate kiss they'd shared, he knew what disaster had happened behind him.

It was his fault. Dammit! All his fault.

His shoulders bunched with guilt, and his nerves frayed from frustration. Not at Sydney. Or Emily. But at himself.

He jerked away from her and raced back to the table. Broken shards of the orange sherbet bowl crunched beneath his shoes. He slipped on a glob of the melting dessert but managed to right himself. Feeling Sydney's heated gaze following after him, he wondered if she was angry at his boldness or irritated at the interruption. Frankly, he felt both emotions vying for control inside him. Until he got a good look at his daughter.

Quiet hummed around him, punctuated by Emily's delighted squeals. It felt as if all the customers in the restaurant along with the wait staff glared at him, irritated at his inability to control his ten-month-old daughter.

Smiling, Emily stood in her high chair, as proud as if she were queen and making a pronouncement. Lifting her hands above her head, she squeezed a scoop of dessert she'd snagged out of the bowl before it fell to the floor. The bright orange goop ran through her chubby fingers and into her hair. A glob dripped off her nose and chin and ran in melting rivulets down her face.

Seeing his daughter teetering precariously on her perch scared the starch right out of Luke. Somehow she'd managed to unfasten the safety strap around her waist and pushed herself up onto her wobbly, uncertain legs. His heart completely stopped.

His daughter wobbled, her arms flailing, her eyes rounding. Luke lunged for her. Not caring about the gooey mess still spotting her hair, her sticky hands, arms and face, he hauled her against him. He wrapped his arms securely around her warm, little body. One hand closed protectively over her tiny arm, the other arm propped up her diapered bottom. He felt her fingers dive into his hair, her hot breath on his cheek, her solid form against him. He sucked in a breath and smelled the distinct scents of baby lotion and orange sherbet. Relief swelled his heart. An overwhelming sense of love crashed over him.

She was safe now, he told himself. Safe.

How easy it had been for him to forget his daughter! Even for a moment. Regret pinched him. He'd been distracted by a set of pretty blue eyes, the color of bluebonnets, and a pair of long, silken legs that should be insured by Lloyds of London. Damn him! He was just like his father.

He rocked from foot to foot, soothing Emily and his own nerves. When he finally felt reassured that she was safe, he reached for a handful of napkins out of the metal dispenser with more force than necessary. Crumpling the wad of roughened paper in his fist, he began mopping up his daughter's mess. He swiped a blotch from beneath her chin, dabbed at the damage done to her dark, downy curls that now looked the color of Pippi Longstocking's ponytails, and swabbed between each finger. Twisting her head and closing her hands into tiny fists, she protested with grunts and stuck her bottom lip out in a decidedly unladylike pout. Her round chocolatey eyes looked up at him dolefully, and he softened his approach.

"You're too busy for your own good, li'l lady," he murmured. "It's bath time for you when we get home."

"I knew we'd all end up spotted like a Dr. Seuss character," Sydney said with a warm chuckle.

He scowled in response. "It looks like this...field trip," he emphasized the purpose of their outing for his, as well as Sydney's, benefit, "will have to end early."

As the waitress arrived with a mop and broom to sweep up the sticky broken glass on the floor, he nodded his thanks and said, "We'll take the baklava with us."

"Sure thing. I'll get you a to-go-box."

Luke figured the waitress would be relieved when they left. Before they coated the entire restaurant in orange sherbet.

With his body still vibrating from Sydney's kiss, he avoided looking in her direction, but knew when she moved her chair out of the way of the waitress's broom. He cursed himself for his stupidity, for his irresponsibility. Damn!

He studied his daughter's sweet face, looking for any last traces of sherbet. Emily could have been hurt. She could have cut herself on the glass. She could have toppled out of the high chair. Anything could have happened. And it would have been his fault. All because he couldn't keep his roving eye off Sydney. Couldn't keep his hands to himself. Couldn't keep his libido under control. What had he been thinking?

Nothing! That was the problem. He had to keep his head

on straight around Sydney. Otherwise, no telling what sort
of a mess he'd get himself into.

Well, it wouldn't happen again. Never!

Tossing the soggy napkins and stained bib in a rumpled
heap on the table, he hugged Emily close again. He
wouldn't let anything happen to her. He wouldn't let himself be distracted. Not by any woman. Especially Sydney.

But it would be an uphill battle all the way. Because
somehow Sydney got under his skin. And that made him
nervous. He couldn't let her affect him, with those soulful
eyes or tales of woe. He had to keep his distance.

Besides, he reminded himself, Sydney wasn't like his
mother who'd needed protection, who'd needed someone
to take care of her. Sydney could take care of herself. He
had no responsibility where she was concerned.

Okay, he owed her help with the desserts for her party
since she'd helped him with Emily. But that was it. That's
where he drew the line. That's where his obligation
stopped.

"Let's go." His voice scratched with raw emotions.

Sydney closed the lid of the squeaky foam to-go-box.
She straightened her narrow skirt, and he caught himself
staring at the shape of her calf, the delicate angle of her
ankle, the shimmer of stockings in the waning evening
light. When she reached for the diaper bag, he cursed himself for his foolishness. Irritated over his obsession with
her, Luke grabbed it first. Their hands brushed. A shimmy
of anticipation shot up his arm once again.

Damn! Sydney was trouble. Trouble he would just have
to avoid. He squelched his reaction to her with firm resolve
and turned toward the exit.

Shock clicked in Sydney's veins like ice cubes in a
chilled glass. Numb, she followed Luke to his car. The sight
of Emily's tiny little hand on his shoulder pinched her

heart. The heat of the summer night pressed down on her like a heavy burden.

She still felt Luke's mouth moving over hers, his breath hot and urgent, her pulse chaotic and racing. With one kiss, which had not lasted nearly long enough, she'd tasted his strength and her own insatiable need. It had shaken her very core.

In that blink of an eye, she'd tried to convince herself it had simply been too long since she'd been kissed with such a charming mixture of tenderness and greed.

She'd absorbed his heat, soaking it up like the earth relishing the sun's warm rays on the first day of spring. His lips had enveloped hers, stealing her breath and setting her on fire. His strength had erased her sorrow and brought a part of her she'd thought dead back to life. His kiss had ignited her soul with a consuming heat. It wouldn't be easily doused.

Her mind felt crazed as she tried to catalogue all the sensations that had assaulted her body. His gentle touch had unnerved her. His clean, crisp scent had aroused her. His taste had mingled with hers in an erotic way that made her think of bodies entwining, sheets tangling. She'd responded to him in an earthy way, needing...wanting...

Then, she'd realized she'd never been kissed *that* way before. By anyone like him. The appalling reality showed her it wasn't the kiss, it was simply Luke.

She'd leaned toward him, eager for more.

But at that precise moment, he'd pulled away.

Had he sensed her need? Had it spooked him? Or had he heard Emily knocking her bowl off the table?

And more important—now what? How would they go back to the platonic relationship they'd shared? Because they had to. She had to help him with Emily, so he would help her with preparing for the baby shower. That's the only reason she didn't call a cab and head home...alone.

Her nerves felt as loose and flimsy as a broken rubber band. She wished Luke would give her some kind of signal, some sign as to what he was thinking. Instead of that deep frown. Did he realize their kiss had been a mistake? Did he regret it as much as she did? If not, then how would she tell him?

Or worse, had he already forgotten their kiss in his worry over his precious baby? That thought made her spine stiffen with resentment. She wouldn't...couldn't forget that kiss. Ever.

Maybe it would be better if he had forgotten about it. Maybe then they wouldn't have to discuss it. Maybe they could just go back to what they'd shared before.

What had they shared? Her brow tightened. They'd shared too much. That had been the problem. She'd spilled her heartache over her divorce. She'd asked too many questions about his childhood. A prickly heat seared her skin, burning its way up her neck and scorching her cheeks.

Walking along busy Greenville Avenue, Sydney squared her shoulders and resisted glancing over at Luke holding Emily. Grateful for the fading light of twilight, she hoped the shadows of night hid the heat of embarrassment on her face. She wouldn't kiss him again. And she certainly wouldn't tell him about her painful past, why her marriage had really failed.

Oh, God! What if she'd told him *everything?* Thank God she hadn't been able to get the words out. She guaranteed herself it wouldn't happen again! But how?

It had been so easy to talk to Luke, so easy to open her heart. But why Luke? Why not somebody...anybody... else? She never shared her problems, never divulged her heartaches. What was the point? With Luke, though, it had been a mutual sharing, as if they'd understood each other, because of their painful childhoods—different yet too similar to ignore.

But there were other things he could never understand. With a glance at Luke and his daughter walking beside her, she felt the painful regrets squeeze her heart.

She'd tried for so long to move beyond the closed doors in her life. But something about Luke, maybe his eagerness to be a good father, maybe Emily's sweetness, made her face those formidable barriers. With regret. With longing. With anger.

She clenched her hands into tight fists. It wasn't fair. It simply wasn't fair! Emily's mother had everything Sydney had ever wanted…a handsome, caring man and a beautiful child. And the woman had thrown it all away. As Sydney grabbed for that dream, the pain constricted her throat and the emptiness in her arms felt more acute.

Luke opened the car door for her, then settled Emily in her car seat in the back. Sydney climbed into his Lexus and strapped on her seat belt. She tried to ignore his closeness when he slid into the driver's seat. She could have reached out and touched his arm, his thigh, his hand. But she wouldn't.

The quiet in the car sounded as loud as gunfire. She heard each breath, each rustle of Emily's diaper as the baby shifted restlessly behind them, and the sound of the engine catching.

Luke pulled out of the parking lot onto the main road and slid a glance toward her. His hands gripped the steering wheel as if he wanted to strangle it. "It should not have happened."

The heat in his statement caught her by surprise. She flinched. She wondered if he referred to Emily sliding the bowl off the table. Or their kiss. She couldn't seem to stop thinking about the way her body had responded to Luke, his kiss. Every fiber in her body had reached out for him with an insatiable need. How would she deny it again? Did she want to?

Yes. It wasn't an easy answer. But it was an impossible question. She couldn't get involved with Luke. She simply wouldn't let him close enough to erase her good sense again with his sexy smile, warm and inviting voice or fiery kiss. For some reason, he made those elusive dreams seem within reach. And she knew that was only a mirage.

Twisting her hands together in her lap, she preferred to think he meant his daughter. After all, wasn't he always talking about Emily? Wasn't he always asking questions about how to raise her? What to do? How to manage? Emily was his first and only concern.

She remembered the tormented look in his eyes as he'd lifted Emily out of the high chair and clutched her to him as if they might be separated forever. A pang had shot through her heart and too many emotions had welled up in her throat.

"Accidents happen," she said, her voice wavering with conviction. Because even though she knew she should never kiss Luke again, she knew she wanted to. Desperately. Her insides trembled with need.

"Not to me." Luke's jaw hardened.

Tightening her grip on reality, she let his words sink in. If he wasn't to blame, then who was? Emily? Who could blame a ten-month-old for stretching her wings? And that left Sydney holding the ticking bomb. Her irritation sharpened on Luke. Who was he to say that accidents didn't happen?

"I see that," she snapped. She gave a pointed look at his daughter in the backseat, the daughter he hadn't planned, the daughter he hadn't known about until last week.

He ground his teeth. "I refuse to think of my daughter as...." He lowered his voice, and it came out like the swish of a blade. "She is not an accident.

"But tonight," he said, his throat working up and down, "I was wrong. Dead wrong."

She knew then he meant the kiss. Her stomach plummeted like a sky diver without a parachute. She couldn't avoid it any longer. She straightened her skirt and wished she could crawl under her seat. "Luke, it happened. Let's not make a whole big deal out of it." She tried for a light, flippant chuckle. "Trust me, I won't make you marry me or anything just because you kissed me."

He turned a sharp gaze on her. "I wasn't talking about the kiss."

His cool, dismissive tone wounded her more than it should have. "I can handle that. I meant, my daughter could have been hurt."

"Oh." She sat a moment, listening to the chaotic beat of her heart, and tried to gather her scattered thoughts. She wrapped her purse's strap around her index finger, pulling it tight, watching the pad swell and grow red with trapped blood. She released the tension with a sigh. "Luke—" she tried to keep her focus on his parenting skills and off the intriguing, rigid lines of his profile and the way his comment had shattered her nerves "—as much as every parent would like to avoid every accident with their child, it's logistically impossible.

"You can't foresee every potential problem. You can't watch them every second of the day." She was talking as fast as her skittering pulse, trying to remind herself to learn from her own mistakes. Like not kissing Luke again! "Accidents will happen. Emily will scrape her knee. You'll patch it up, give her a kiss, and go on." She stared at the long street of red and green lights ahead of them and wished he'd drive faster, get her home sooner. "With each incident, you'll learn. So will she. You can't protect her from life. Making mistakes is part of her learning process, too."

She felt her face burning. Maybe if she kept talking, he wouldn't notice. Then he wouldn't disregard the kiss they'd shared as something trite or inconsequential. As silly as it sounded in her own mind, she knew it had meant more than it should have.

"You have to remember—" she managed to keep her voice from trembling like her stomach "—that most parents start out with a tiny infant that sleeps most of the time. So the potential for accidents is less."

She slanted her gaze toward him. He seemed to be listening. At least he wasn't speaking. The tension in his jaw had begun to relax. Shifting her gaze back to the road, she prayed they arrived quickly. Before she ran out of things to say.

"But remember," she said, "your baby came to you already crawling and grabbing. It'll take a little while for you to catch up with her growth and her abilities. Soon, going out to a restaurant will be as simple as tying your shoes. You won't even have to think about it."

He glanced at her for a heart-stopping moment, his eyes seemed to swallow all glimmers of light, then he shifted his gaze back to the road ahead. "Maybe. Maybe you were right. The real problem was that kiss."

Her stomach rolled in a sick free-for-all.

"If that hadn't happened," he continued, "then Emily wouldn't have almost been hurt. It was reckless. Stupid."

She felt the sharp jab of his words into her heart. He acted like it was her fault! Like she'd kissed him! She wanted to shove aside their kiss and keep the focus on Luke and his daughter, but she knew she had to face the discussion like a problem at work—head-on.

"Look, Luke, I admit it wasn't the best timing. You caught me by surprise. But let's not make it a federal case. What you said is right. Emily could have been hurt. But she *wasn't*. That's what is important."

"It's a symptom, Sydney. I have to make sure it won't happen again."

Defensive, she crossed her arms over her chest. "It won't."

"You can't guarantee that. Not with us working together." He shoved his hand through his hair and slumped back in his seat.

"Then there's only one solution." Her throat burned. Maybe it was for the best. If so, then why did it hurt so much? Why did she suddenly feel lost without him? "Maybe we should call off our agreement."

"I don't know.... I don't seem to know anything anymore. Especially what I need to know to be a good father."

She resisted placing her hand on his arm. She fought back the sympathy that seemed to automatically respond to him. Instead, she spoke from her heart. "Sure you do. You know how to change diapers. You know how to clean up Emily's messes. And you're learning how to avoid certain disasters-in-the-making.

"It's not so much what you *do*, it's whether or not you care, whether or not you love your daughter that makes you a good father or not. Believe me, I can see how much you love Emily."

When he glanced in her direction, she felt suddenly vulnerable, as if she'd said too much. She stared at the red light they were approaching and pushed her foot against the floorboard as he pressed on the brake. She put a stop to her feelings of regret. Luke was right. They should slam on the brakes right now. Before it was too late.

"I need your help." His lips tightened to a narrow line. He stared at the taillights of the car ahead of them.

"You could find someone else." But could she?

He stretched open his hands along the steering wheel then gripped it until the tendons and muscles along his fingers and wrists knotted and flexed. Shaking his head, he cursed under his breath. She sensed a frustration and self-incrimination churning inside him. He looked into the rear-view mirror, and the corner of his mouth quirked. "Emily's asleep."

"Too much excitement for one night." For Sydney, too! She felt her own energy draining away with each minute and wished she were already at home, curled up in bed with a boring book that would put her to sleep. So she wouldn't have to think anymore. But she knew she'd dream...about that kiss...about Luke.

She wondered what was going on inside Luke's head. Why couldn't he simply say he wouldn't kiss her again and be done with it? Did he think she wanted him so much that she'd throw herself at him? A flare of anger arced through her. She'd set him straight on that right away.

"Look, Luke, if you're worried about me attacking you for another kiss or tempting you to stray from your fatherly duties, then don't. I didn't ask for the kiss. I don't want it to happen again either. The last thing I want is a relationship. My work is too important." Better to let him continue comparing her to Emily's mother, Sydney thought, her chest aching.

"Quit saying that."

Taken back by the ferocity in his voice, she said, "What?"

"That you're so damn career-oriented."

She straightened her spine. "Well, it's true. I'm not just saying that, hoping to rope you in later."

"I know. But...damn! I can tell you mean it. I learned a long time ago to read between the lines. But the trouble is..."

She waited for him to continue, well aware that her heart was pounding. When he didn't finish, she finally prodded him with, "What?"

He released a heavy sigh. "I've always been attracted to

women who claimed they didn't want a relationship. I don't know why." He paused, the silence stretching as he urged the car forward with a gentle touch on the gas. She guessed he wanted someone different from his mother, someone strong, confident, determined. Who better than a career-oriented woman? "Maybe," he finally said, "because then I didn't have to face the truth."

"Which was?"

His face contorted. His throat contracted, the muscles stretching over his Adam's apple. He drove past three street lights before he answered.

"That I'm like my father." He turned the wheel, steering his car onto her street, his hands sure and strong, but his voice sounded rough with defeat.

Surprised, she shifted to look at him more fully. She remembered her own father's loving embrace, his weathered brow puckered with concern, his willingness to talk late into the night when she had a problem. Most of all, she treasured the memory of his tears, the way he'd sobbed at her mother's funeral, holding tightly to all four of his kids, needing them for reassurance. She remembered the way he'd sniffed back tears of pride, joy and sorrow at her wedding and the horrible way he'd cried with her when she'd told him the reason for her divorce.

It amazed and appalled her that someone hadn't grown up with a father like her own. Sadness tightened her throat. This time, she couldn't resist the impulse to place a comforting hand on his arm. She felt the tension in his bunched muscles resist her. She sensed the discomfort in him reacting to her compassion. And she detected something more...something she didn't want to consider...a response in herself that she wouldn't allow.

"How are you like your father?" she asked, needing something to fill the silence between them, the emptiness in her heart.

He ran a hand through his tousled hair and expelled a weary breath. "My dad was not a good man. It used to hurt me to say that. But it's the truth. I knew it from the time I was a child. The first time he hurt my mother."

Horror filled her mind. Her hand tightened on his arm, felt the restrained strength, the gentle warmth. "Did he hit her?"

"No. But the scars couldn't have been any more real. He had one affair after another."

Her heart flinched, knowing the pain, shame and disgust she'd felt at her own husband's infidelities. Anger filled her mouth with a biting taste of revulsion. "That's why he left?"

Luke nodded. "He found a younger woman." His hand balled into a fist. "One without the burden of a kid."

As he parked in front of Sydney's apartment, he turned to face her. Shadows made his eyes look hooded, haunted. The slant of a parking light cut across the plain of his cheek and gave his features a sharp angle. "Sydney, I was wrong. I shouldn't have kissed you. I-I don't know why—"

"That's not important," she said, not wanting to hear his excuses, his reasons. Her own were staggering enough. She glanced down at her hand on his arm. Feeling awkward, as if she'd crossed an invisible barrier, and sensing what was about to be said, she pulled her hand away and held it against her middle.

"Maybe not. But I'm not looking for a relationship. Of any kind. I never have wanted marriage. Not after watching my mom and dad..." His voice trailed off into a palpable silence.

She watched his jaw work, the muscles and tendons tightening and flexing along the square bone. She sensed powerful emotions churning inside him and put her hand on the car door, ready to escape, needing to leave before she did something foolish, like try to comfort him again.

NO POSTAGE
NECESSARY
IF MAILED
IN THE
UNITED STATES

BUSINESS REPLY MAIL
FIRST-CLASS MAIL   PERMIT NO. 717   BUFFALO, NY

POSTAGE WILL BE PAID BY ADDRESSEE

SILHOUETTE READER SERVICE
3010 WALDEN AVE
PO BOX 1867
BUFFALO NY 14240-9952

The Silhouette Reader Service™ — Here's how it works:

Accepting your 2 free books and mystery gift places you under no obligation to buy anything. You may keep the books and gift and return the shipping statement marked "cancel." If you do not cancel, about a month later we'll send you 6 additional novels and bill you just $3.90 each in the U.S., or $3.25 each in Canada, plus 25¢ delivery per book and applicable taxes if any.* That's the complete price and — compared to the cover price of $3.50 in the U.S. and $3.99 in Canada — it's quite a bargain! You may cancel at any time, but if you choose to continue, every month we'll send you 6 more books, which you may either purchase at the discount price or return it to us and cancel your subscription.

*Terms and prices subject to change without notice. Sales tax applicable in N.Y. Canadian residents will be charged applicable provincial taxes and GST.

NO RISK, NO OBLIGATION TO BUY…NOW OR EVER!

GUARANTEED

PLAY "ROLL A DOUBLE"
AND YOU GET FREE GIFTS!

HERE'S HOW TO PLAY:

1. Peel off label from front cover. Place it in space provided at right. With a coin, carefully scratch off the silver dice. Then check the claim chart to see what we have for you – TWO FREE BOOKS and a mystery gift – ALL YOURS! ALL FREE!

2. Send back this card and you'll receive brand-new Silhouette Romance® novels. These books have a cover price of $3.50 each in the U.S. and $3.99 each in Canada, but they are yours to keep absolutely free.

3. There's no catch. You're under no obligation to buy anything. We charge nothing – ZERO – for your first shipment. And you don't have to make any minimum number of purchases – not even one!

4. The fact is, thousands of readers enjoy receiving books by mail from the Silhouette Reader Service™. They like the convenience of home delivery…they like getting the best new novels BEFORE they're available in stores…and they love our discount prices!

5. We hope that after receiving your free books you'll want to remain a subscriber. But the choice is yours – to continue or cancel any time at all! So why not take us up on our invitation, with no risk of any kind. You'll be glad you did!

"I always cursed my dad for the way he treated my mother. Maybe I knew instinctively. Maybe it was fear. I don't know. But tonight, I realized I inherited my father's genes."

Her stomach gave a sickening turn. "What do you mean?"

He sighed. "Sydney, you've got to know you're very attractive...a beautiful woman. You've been kind to help me with Emily. You have a good heart. But you distracted me tonight from my daughter. It's not you. I'm not blaming you in any way. But it showed me that I could easily walk away from my own responsibilities and commitments. And I won't let that happen.

"So, tonight," he met her shocked gaze squarely, his eyes deep and dark and filled with angst, "that kiss, can't be repeated. Do you understand?"

Anger snapped inside her. Hadn't she made herself clear?

Then something in his soft gaze, the sadness, the honesty, tugged at her heart. Finally she understood. He wasn't blaming her. He was blaming himself. He was stating it for his benefit. To boost his resolve.

Which meant he wanted to kiss her again. As much as she wanted to kiss him. And her heart rolled completely over.

Her irritation and anger gave way to respect. This man, this brand-new father, had honor, integrity and a level of devotion that seemed rare in this day and age. She doubted his professed inability to commit. She'd witnessed his devotion to his daughter, his willingness to turn his life upside down to accommodate her needs. He was already a wonderful father to Emily. Why couldn't he see that?

Someday, she knew, he'd make a loving, caring husband to some lucky lady. That thought made her freeze.

Not *her* husband. That wasn't possible!

Even though she liked Luke, respected him, it was simply impossible. Their lives were heading in different directions. She was on her way to a good career, and she wouldn't let some guy like Luke derail her efforts.

As much as she liked Emily, she'd already raised someone else's kids. This was her time to be selfish, to spread her own wings. And no man would ever clip them again.

"I understand what you're saying, Luke. It's okay. I'm not interested in a relationship either. Let's just be friends." She drew her bottom lip between her teeth. Uncertainty made her nerves rattle. "I don't mind advising you on how to raise Emily. If you don't mind helping me make some desserts."

She gave him a shy smile. "Would you like to come up and taste the baklava we didn't get around to tonight?"

He shook his head. "I better get Emily home, cleaned up and into bed. We'll try out another recipe tomorrow."

She nodded. It was the right answer. It was the only answer. Her gaze dropped to his mouth. She knew she wouldn't receive a good-night kiss. Not that she needed one. His last and only kiss would linger in her mind for a long time to come.

She yanked on the door handle, but his hand touched her arm. A current of electricity pulsed through her body with anticipation. "Thanks, Sydney, for listening. I, um, don't usually talk so much."

"Neither do I," she confessed, feeling a heady warmth move through her.

Luke's sensitivity, his pain and his too-darn-sexy smile would be the devil to resist. But she would. She had to.

Chapter Six

Where was she?

Luke's heart skipped a beat. He stood in the kitchen as numbness slid over his body. Suddenly, he felt all alone. Isolated in his own house. Uncomfortable with his concern for Sydney, he shoved his hands in his jeans pockets. Damn. When had he started to look forward to these quiet evenings with her?

Almost since the beginning.

At first, it had been hope that she'd help him with Emily. But now, it was much more. Too much.

A week had passed since the disaster at the dessert place...and their kiss. They hadn't mentioned it again. Immediately, there had been an awkwardness between them with stiff gestures, quick sidelong glances, and avoiding even brushing shoulders. They'd concentrated on Emily, baklava and chocolate soufflé. They'd discussed the best diaper brands, sifting flour and separating eggs until they'd learned to anticipate each other's needs—a pacifier, spatula or pinch of salt. They'd become a team.

But in the back of his mind...or maybe too often in the forefront...he'd thought about that kiss.

Turning on his heel, he grabbed a handful of his own hair and wondered where she'd gone. He'd left her here in the kitchen while he went to put Emily down for the night. He'd only been gone twenty minutes. Sydney had said she'd start on the chocolate mousse but the aluminum bowl lay empty on the counter. Beside it, the eggs still sat in the carton and the sugar remained in the plastic container. Had she gotten bored? Irritated? Had she left? When he saw her purse still lying on the kitchen counter, he breathed easier.

Then he saw her. And his lungs contracted.

Through the windows, along the back of his house, the glass reflected the pool water rippling in the twilight. She sat on the edge of the pool, her bare feet dangling in the water. The glow of the sun caught the golden-and-ruby highlights in her hair. A faint breeze molded her blouse to her breasts. She squinted toward the waning sun as it crashed to earth on its descent. It was the most beautiful sunset he'd ever seen.

All because of Sydney.

He rubbed a hand over his eyes, trying to erase the image from his mind...from his heart. But he knew it was a wasted motion. Sydney had carved a place for herself in his memory. It was dangerous, he conceded. But then again, he rationalized, as he ran through the same old argument he'd used when telling Sydney he didn't want a relationship, maybe it wasn't.

He wasn't ignoring his daughter. She was safely tucked in bed. He wasn't endangering Emily, not like when he'd walked away from her in a high chair. He was simply enjoying the sight of a beautiful woman—Sydney. She'd come to mean more to him in the last couple of weeks than she should have.

But he couldn't ignore the effect she had on him. He

couldn't deny that he enjoyed their evenings together. As long as it didn't take anything away from his daughter, then he figured it was okay. Wasn't it?

He opened the French doors and joined her at poolside. She looked up at him, giving him an engaging smile that lit her eyes with the twinkle of stardust. His heart kicked into high gear and pummeled his rib cage. Blood roared in his ears. He felt like a gangly teenager as he dropped to the deck beside her.

Her light, flowery scent drifted to him on a soft breeze. His abs tightened with the effort to squash the effect she was having on him. He wondered what damage she could do to him if she really tried to turn him on. Feeling as though he should have stayed in the kitchen and kept a yardstick's distance between them, he gave her a wry, self-deprecating smile and managed in a strangled voice, "Nice evening."

"Hmm." She gazed at the distant horizon. "Beautiful."

His thoughts exactly. But he wasn't looking at the sunset. Instead, he noticed the faint freckles along Sydney's delicately shaped nose, the fine angle of her jaw, the gentle slope of her cheek. He wanted to edge closer, study her, memorize every nuance that made Sydney uniquely her. Adhering to the voice of reason, weak though it was, he punished himself by squinting against the last harsh rays of the sun.

"Did Emily go down easily?" she asked, her voice as soothing as the water lapping against her calves.

He nodded. "She's sleeping like a…"

Sydney looked at him then and smiled, making tiny dimples appear on either side of her mouth and causing his stomach to contract. "Baby?"

A reluctant chuckle rumbled in his chest. "Makes sense, I guess, since she is one. But it's taken Emily a while to realize that's what she was supposed to do."

"It'll get easier," she said.

"If it gets any more difficult," he laughed, "then go ahead and bury me now. Because I won't survive."

"Sure you will. This is the hazing period of parenthood."

"I thought hazing was illegal."

"Not for kids." Her smile softened with sympathy and a good dose of humor. "If you can survive this, then there's a good chance you'll survive puberty."

He groaned. A long stretch of single parenthood stretched out before him like the Yellow Brick Road. It held promise. But it looked lonely as it traveled through dark, dense forests of unknown obstacles. Could he walk it alone? Could he manage on his own?

He felt his throat constrict. "You should have seen Em tonight. While I was feeding her, she placed her hand on mine as I held the bottle."

"Soon, she'll be able to hold the bottle herself."

He felt strange emotions tug on his heart. He wasn't ready for that. Each night, he felt the bond between him and his daughter grow stronger. He didn't want her pushing away from him yet. But he knew someday soon she would. Then, he'd be all alone again. "She spoke."

Sydney raised her brows, and a secretive smile lurked on her lips. "What'd she say?"

"It's probably nothing," he said, doubting suddenly what he'd heard come out of his daughter's mouth. "Most of the time, she's talking in some foreign language. Babbling."

"Baby gibberish," Sydney added with a nod of understanding.

"But tonight..." His throat squeezed shut with powerful emotions that choked him. "Tonight, she said, 'da-da.'"

"Oh, Luke," Sydney said, placing a hand on his arm, "how wonderfully sweet."

His skin, where she touched him, tingled. His nerves tangled like a ball of fishing twine. At least she hadn't said he was imagining things. She hadn't given him an excuse that all babies made those sounds. For that, for the understanding she showed him, he was forever grateful.

When he looked into her eyes, he knew she grasped the magnitude of the moment he'd shared with his daughter. A smile stretched his mouth wide, and he felt his heart swell with joy. "It was the greatest feeling in the world."

She gave a gentle squeeze to his arm, and his heart contracted. Then she slowly pulled her hand away. But in that moment, in that instant, he knew he didn't want to walk that long road into the future alone. As he'd been able to tell Sydney of that powerful exchange with his daughter, he wanted to share the sweet moments when Emily walked by herself, said her first coherent words and headed off to kindergarten. He wanted to share the painful moments of disappointment and sorrow. He wanted to share the frustrations, the questions, the worry.

With regret, he knew Emily's biological mother wouldn't be around for advice, comfort or experiencing those poignant moments of watching their daughter grow into adulthood. He'd made a mistake getting involved with her. But he couldn't whole-heartedly regret that time either. Not when he'd been blessed with a beautiful baby girl.

But who would want to share the moments ahead? Who would care as much as he did about his baby girl? Who would ever understand how this little baby could make his heart surge with pride and joy?

Beside him, he felt Sydney's reassuring support. A comfortable silence settled between them as the last full rays of light faded and darkness crept over them. Luke held his breath, wanting this time with Sydney to go on and on. He wondered then if she could care enough about Emily...about *him*... to join him on this adventure.

Then he shoved that thought aside. He was being too sentimental, too frivolous. Did he really want to get married? Did he want to share Emily, take time away from his daughter?

As clear as the rising moon, he remembered Sydney's comments about relationships and marriage. She wouldn't want him or Emily. She wouldn't want to share the heartache and triumphs. She wouldn't want to be a part of their lives, a part of their family. A chilling breeze wafted over him, making the empty place in his heart seem deeper and colder than before.

"Do you come out here often?" she asked, her tranquil voice interrupting his thoughts. "It's so peaceful."

Confused by his own questions and the acute disappointment he felt knowing Sydney wouldn't be interested in a relationship, he gave a slight shrug. "Not enough. Before Emily, I was too busy with the restaurant. Now that she's here, I'm too busy with her."

She reached down and tapped the top of the water with her fingertips. Tiny concentric circles rippled outward through the pool. "What are you going to do?"

Irritated suddenly at Sydney, at her persistent questions, at the strange feelings wrapping around his heart, he snapped, "I put the restaurant up for sale."

She shifted to look at him. Her foot popped out of the water and made a splash. "What?"

He noticed in that instant, even in the dim light, that her toenails were painted red. Part of him wanted to glimpse her toes again. Part of him wanted to forget he'd ever seen her toes or tasted this woman's intoxicating kiss. Annoyed by her, his reaction to her, and the romantic setting produced by the full moon and glittering stars, he crossed his arms over his chest.

"It's not that big a deal." And he meant it. Putting the Iron-horse Brewery on the block hadn't hurt as badly as he'd anticipated. In fact, it had brought a significant amount of relief. Now, if it would sell quickly.

"But it was your life."

"Now, Emily is," he said, simply, honestly. "Things change." As he knew he had. His hopes, dreams and desires had changed. "Someday, if I want I can open a new one. The sale will give us plenty to live on for a while. Until I figure out what else I can do."

"You mean like a boring nine-to-five job?" She shook her head. "I can't see you wearing a suit and carrying a briefcase."

"Me, either. And I can't see myself carting Emily to day care every day. I want something I can do at home. Where I can take care of my daughter and attend to business. I don't want to waste these precious years of Emily's life."

As surely as he'd felt her hand on his arm earlier, he felt Sydney studying him. Clasping his hands together, he leaned forward, propping his elbows on his bent knees. He studied the calluses along the inside of his palm. He refused to look at her, to see contempt or, worse, pity, in her eyes. He didn't want to hear arguments against what he'd decided. He wanted...needed...her support, her understanding. Because he felt as if he'd stepped out on a limb.

However, in his gut, he knew he'd made the right choice. No one could change his mind about that. Not a woman. Not Sydney. And certainly not a disparaging glance. To prove his confidence in his own decision, he slid his gaze toward her. Then he regretted it.

The lights from inside his house caught the tears welling in her eyes, making the blue depths look like waves in the ocean. "That's the bravest, most caring thing I've ever heard anyone do." Her voice grew husky and stirred a new batch of emotions inside him. "Emily is a lucky little girl to have you for a father."

Luke's throat squeezed tight. "It was the only thing I could do."

"No." She shook her head sadly. "There were a million things you could have done. But you made the right decision. I admire you for that. Not everyone is that strong."

He'd wanted support, but her admiration made him uneasy and muddled his thinking. He stood, awkward, silent. But he felt less alone, knowing she approved. Slowly, not knowing what else to do, he offered his hand to her. "Ready to go in?"

She placed her cool fingertips against his palm, and he clasped her hand. Heat flared between them. Their eyes met. His stomach did a free fall into a deep pit of uncertainty.

"Want to try it again?" His suggestive statement lingered between them like an invitation. He'd meant their next recipe. Or had he? Instinctively, he felt a hum of electricity between them. Immediately, he thought of the kiss they'd shared.

Over the last week, he'd thought of that kiss way too much. At night, lying in his king-size bed all alone, he'd remembered the sweet taste of her mouth, the incredible softness of her lips, like sugar melting in the rain. During the day, when he'd been busy with Emily, picking up her toys, he'd held his daughter's well-loved lamb and considered Sydney's gentleness, her encouraging touch, the innocent yet knowing blush on her cheeks.

Each thought unraveled his nerves, unsettled his peace of mind. But when he rocked his daughter to sleep each night, he'd realized how quiet the house seemed, how alone he'd be after Emily went to bed. A part of him hadn't wanted that anymore.

He'd wanted to walk out of Emily's bedroom and find Sydney waiting for him. As he had tonight. He wanted to share sunsets with this woman. He wanted to hold her hand. He wanted to kiss her again and again. But for how long?

And his insides clenched with self-reproach.

Her face flushed in the soft glow of moonlight, making her eyes sparkle with a mischievous light. "If you think we're ready."

He cleared his throat and erased his crazy thoughts. "I do."

But he knew he wasn't ready for what his heart longed for. He didn't know if he'd ever be. Not that he would hurt Sydney...or his daughter by taking a plunge into deep, dark waters.

He knew they were ready to try their hand at a mousse, soufflé and crème brûlée, not another kiss, certainly not a relationship.

Sydney's brow wrinkled. She concentrated on the mocha taste and smooth, airy texture lingering in her mouth. With the tip of her tongue, she swiped the last dollop of mousse off the spoon. Luke's steady gaze focused on her and set fire to her cheeks. He stared at her mouth. Self-conscious, she rolled her lips inward to avoid checking with her tongue for any remaining specks of the creamy mixture. The silence hung between them like a pendulum. His anticipation of her verdict deepened the lines around his dark, serious eyes.

To lighten the mood and ease the tension twisting her insides with racy thoughts, she said, "Not bad."

"Not bad?" He stepped back and shoved his fingers through his already tousled hair. "This is the third mousse in a week. It doesn't get better than this. You're too hard to please."

"I'm a perfectionist, I know, but I'm not hard to please." She thought of exactly what he could do to please her, and her skin tightened with the need for his touch.

"What's wrong with the mousse this time?" he asked, his voice brusque.

"Nothing." She smiled, and nervous laughter bubbled out of her. "I was teasing. It's yummy."

His frown lifted. "You think it'll pass then?"

"You'll have all the women drooling at the shower." She was drooling now. And it had nothing to do with the sumptuous dessert.

"I won't be there."

A ball of realization stuck in her throat. "Of course. What I meant was that...uh..." Her face burned with awareness. "This m-mousse will, um, wow my guests." Her hand trembled as she scooped another spoonful. "You're right, of course. I won't need you there. That's what these cooking lessons are for. I can do this."

She swallowed another creamy bite and doubts assailed her. What if she couldn't make this on her own? She had to admit, Luke helped more than she did with Emily. "No, I can't..."

"Sure you can." He patted her shoulder with the flat palm of his hand. It was an awkward attempt to alleviate her concerns. When she met his dark gaze, he turned away abruptly. "You'll be ready. I didn't help much this time."

"Yes, you did. You always help. I feel like I'm the chef's assistant."

"Okay, then let's try this. Let's make something else. And you make it. All by yourself. I'll be here...just watching. You can ask questions, but I won't lift a finger."

Great. Luke watching her would be enough to distract her! With his hooded gaze making her nerve endings sizzle, she'd probably pour in a cup of salt instead of sugar. An excruciating headache pounded her temples. Tension knotted her nerves, and her neck started to ache.

Then suddenly she felt Luke's hands on her shoulders. Heat shot through her. Her stomach clenched. "Easy," he said, his voice as thick as taffy. He kneaded her shoulders, rolling his hands along her muscles, like a chef working bread dough, with confidence, assurance and warmth. "Relax."

His knuckles made light popping sounds as his fingers massaged her stiff neck. Despite her resolve to resist her attraction to him, she felt her body become loose, her knees weaken. She wished he'd go on forever, giving her this sweet torture. And she wished he'd stop before she turned, wrapped her arms around him and kissed him right here in his kitchen!

"Okay," she said, her voice as jumpy as her nerves. "What should I make?"

"What do you think you're ready for?"

You!

She shook her head and took a self-protective step away from him. Lifting her shoulders, she realized his efforts had helped ease the tension in her muscles. "Thanks," she whispered.

"Anytime."

She swallowed hard and wished that were true. She placed a hand over her uneasy stomach. "Maybe something not so rich."

"A non-rich dessert? Is there such a thing?"

"I don't know." Then a funny idea occurred to her. "You know what sounds good? Plain, ol', ordinary brownies."

His grin broadened. "You can do that. Easy."

She nodded. This would resurrect her confidence. Maybe she'd started out with too high expectations. Maybe she should have started with something simpler. "Do you have a recipe?"

"I've got one of my mother's...somewhere." He rummaged in a drawer, pulling pliers, a hammer, stacks of receipts and game pieces from McDonald's out onto the counter. At the bottom, he found a yellowed index card. "Here. You start mixing, I'll get the ingredients out for you."

"Shouldn't I do this all by myself?"

"Setting flour on the counter won't take away from your efforts. But it'll save time. You won't waste time searching my cabinets. And the sooner we get these made, the sooner we can eat them." He rubbed his flat belly. "I'm starved."

She laughed and reached for the nearest mixing bowl. While Luke pulled the ingredients out of his pantry and hunted down measuring spoons and cups, she glanced over the recipe. Each time his arm brushed hers or he reached past her to open the refrigerator and grab a carton of eggs, he distracted her. Why did his roomy kitchen suddenly feel the size of a matchbox? Her nerves tingled with awareness. Her pulse pounded with uncertainty. She tried to concentrate on scooping out the right amount of sugar and dumping it into the bowl, but a clump landed on the counter.

"Stop." Luke stood in the middle of the kitchen with half the cabinets open. "We don't have any cocoa. No use making brownies without the chocolate."

She smiled. "Don't worry. I have some in my car."

His eyebrows slanted downward. "In your car? Why would you carry cocoa? Or are you always this prepared?"

She laughed. "I'm not psychic. I bought both the powdered cocoa and the chocolate squares for the mousse because I couldn't remember which kind I needed. When I got to my car, I looked at the recipe again."

"Chocolate squares," they said in unison.

Smiling, she added, "Yep. So I left the cocoa in the car."

"Okay, then, I'll go get it." In a moment, he was back, cocoa in hand.

To distract herself from his potent masculinity, which seemed hotter than the oven she'd set to three hundred and fifty degrees, she asked, "Have you thought of what you're going to do for a career, once your restaurant sells? Do chefs consult?"

"I suppose. But that would require traveling more." He opened the canister and a puff of chocolate smoke rose. She breathed in the rich scent, monentarily distracted from Luke.

She reached for the can, and their fingers brushed. An electric current surged up her arm. She jerked her hand away and refused to look at his inquisitive glance. Instead, she grabbed the plastic measuring spoons. While he held the canister for her, she spooned out six tablespoons of cocoa. His warm breath drifted over her like a summer breeze, and her hand trembled, knocking granules of cocoa onto the counter.

"I've been thinking about a mail order catalog," he said, his voice contemplative. She wondered if he wanted advice. Or if he was still questioning himself.

Intrigued with his idea, she glanced at him and realized he stood too close to her. Her breath caught in her throat. Her focus shifted to his mouth. How easy it would be to close the gap and taste him again. Her body yearned for another kiss. But she resisted. Her sanity demanded it. She stared at his Adam's apple instead of that wide, intriguing mouth.

"With cooking utensils?" she managed. Her voice sounded smothered by her desire, need and longing to be closer to him.

"Maybe a few." He spoke slowly, as if in a trance. She felt the heat of his gaze on her, touching her lowered eyelids, her cheeks, her lips. Her stomach tumbled over itself. "But mostly with food items."

She shook off her reaction to him, shivering as if the temperature had suddenly dropped. She concentrated on stirring the mixture in the bowl, mixing the eggs, oil and dry ingredients. "All ready."

"Hmm?" His gaze slowly shifted from her mouth to the bowl of brownies. "Oh, you need a pan."

She nodded, as her heart beat its way to her throat and prevented her from speaking.

Luke held a greased pan as she poured the brownie mixture into it. Together, they put it in the oven and set the timer.

"So, your catalog wouldn't necessarily be geared toward chefs," she said, taking them back to a safe topic.

He leaned against the island, his elbow resting on the chopping-block counter. "It'd be targeted at single fathers." His voice sounded full of life and hope and promise.

"That's a great idea!" She felt his enthusiasm beating inside her. "I'm sure there are a lot of other single fathers, whether they're weekend dads or full-time ones, that could use the help." Ideas and possibilities spun around her head, but Luke's very presence made it difficult to concentrate.

"You think this would work?" Uncertainty darkened his eyes.

"Of course. Why wouldn't it? As far as I know there's nothing else serving that market in that particular way."

"True. I'd envisioned there being tips for meals. Of course, there needs to be a recipe book. Simplified for most dads with meals that most kids like. With a list of things to keep in a pantry. Maybe the recipe book could be put on CD-ROM for those computer geeks out there."

"That would be terrific. A dad could search for something at the office before heading home for the night with the kids."

"Exactly!"

She smiled at his enthusiasm, and her pulse thrummed. "What kind of food items would you include?"

"Boxed items that could be easily shipped. A hurried father would only have to add chicken or beef or maybe water. All the ingredients would be in the box."

Teasing, she propped a hand on her hip. "I thought you told me that's not really cooking?"

"A single father doesn't want to cook. It's a necessity. He's not trying for the same effect you are with your shower."

"That's true."

"Life as a single father can be overwhelming."

"You're learning that as we speak."

He nodded. "Later, we could expand to perishable items that can be shipped. Maybe specialty birthday cakes. Cookies."

"You have to start with something you can manage and give yourself room to grow."

"You're right." The buzzer sounded. He grinned, a smile that made her heart turn over. "Brownie time."

He turned off the buzzer but before he opened the oven door, he turned to her. She almost bumped into him and pulled back abruptly. He gazed down at her for a long moment, staring deeply into her eyes. Her heart kicked in response.

"Thanks," he said, his voice thick with emotion, his eyes dark with sincerity.

"For what?" She placed a hand over her thumping heart.

"For liking my idea."

"I love it, Luke." Her throat burned with suppressed emotions.

The tips of his ears turned red with pleasure. "Good. Others haven't been as supportive."

"Who...why?"

"I don't know why. Who's not really important. But..." His Adam's apple jerked beneath the taut skin of his neck. "I value your opinion. And appreciate your support."

"I have no doubts you'll be successful."

"I don't know about that. There's a lot of things I have to figure out. Like the cost of start-up."

"I could help you with the figures," she volunteered before she could think better of it. "After all, I am an accountant."

He grinned. "Good. I'll take you up on that. I could use someone to crunch numbers."

His smile was contagious and warmed her heart. "What are you going to call it?"

"Don't laugh, but I was thinking of Father..." He held up the spice jar "...Thyme. What do you think?"

"Perfect."

He opened the oven door and she pulled out the pan of... She blinked hard. The "brownies" formed a dark wave, rolling with her movements. "How long were we supposed to cook these?"

She checked the recipe. "It's time." Her confidence plummeted. "It's not supposed to look like this, is it?"

"Not usually."

He stirred a spoon through the thick, gooey mess. "Did you by any chance forget to add the flour?"

Her startled gaze flew to meet his then to the full canister on the counter. "Oh, no."

And she knew why she'd forgotten the most important ingredient. Luke. He'd distracted her again.

Chapter Seven

Her fingers moved with graceful assurance, mesmerizing Luke with their precision and skill. For a second, he wished he was the keyboard of her calculator, to feel her hands moving over him. He should focus on the figures appearing on the narrow, white tape but he could only watch Sydney. A small wrinkle appeared in her smooth brow as she plugged in the calculations. She squinted at the legal pad on which he'd jotted notes.

Since she'd volunteered to help him crunch numbers, he'd made calls over the last week to learn more about how to start Father Thyme. The amount of money needed staggered him.

Equally astonishing had been the first offer made on the Iron-horse Brewery. It would provide food, shelter and comfort for a long while. He'd put enough away for Emily's college education and possibly her future wedding. But he couldn't think about that yet. First, he'd save enough to establish security for Emily. Then, he'd use the rest to start his business.

"That much?" Luke looked over Sydney's shoulder. He leaned close and squinted at the numbers. Her powdery, ethereal scent rose to meet him and turned him inside out. He swallowed hard and tried to concentrate on the dollar amount she'd figured. "I didn't realize..." Snapped out of the hazy fog, he blinked. "Jeez! How could anyone afford that?"

Sydney tapped her fingers lightly on the keypad of her calculator. "The problem is the catalog itself. It's a huge investment, the productions costs, the photographs needed, not to mention design, printing and postage costs. All this is right up front, without any guarantees of sales."

"The items will sell," he stated with more confidence than he felt. His stomach twisted like a wrung out wet dishrag. What if the whole company crashed and burned? What if their savings went up in smoke? Doubts burned into his thinking like a red-hot skewer. Could he take that kind of chance with Emily's future?

He'd had doubts before but they didn't usually paralyze him. He'd doubted the wisdom of opening the Iron-horse Brewery. Many of his friends had warned him of the dangers, obstacles and headaches. But he'd believed in his own abilities, in his dream. And it had somehow, miraculously worked.

Now, he had Emily to consider. He couldn't make a leap without it affecting her. What if his company folded? What if he lost his investment? The yoke of parental responsibility tightened around his neck.

He watched Emily play in her playpen, gnawing on the different toys he'd placed along the cushioned floor. His heart swelled with an overwhelming joy. He loved his daughter more than he'd ever thought it possible to love anyone. With each day, his love for her grew and his heart's capacity expanded. Suddenly, the heavy burden of responsibility felt lighter.

He smiled as his daughter banged her lamb against her thigh. He realized going for his own dreams wasn't as selfish as he'd begun to think. As long as he didn't act recklessly. Or forget his responsibilities. Having watched his mother overcome her own fears, he understood that pursuing his own dreams would show Emily that she could chase her own someday. It was the greatest gift, besides love, that he could give his daughter.

"You okay?" she asked, glancing up from the calculator.

He nodded. "I know this sounds impossible. But there has to be a way to figure it out. To make it work.

"Like you've done. You're making your dreams come true." His statement seemed to flap in the space between them, like underwear on a clothesline.

"What?" she asked, her brow furrowing.

Beside him, Emily scrambled on all fours across the playpen, babbling contentedly. Luke struggled within himself to find the words to explain what it meant to him to be Emily's father.

Shifting his attention back to the calculations, he felt an urge to share his thoughts with Sydney. Usually, he kept his feelings to himself, but for some reason it had always been easy, almost natural, to tell Sydney his doubts, fears and hopes. He didn't pause to analyze why.

He sat on the edge of the couch. "You finished your degree. Survived a sour marriage. And pursued your dreams—your career. By doing that, you showed your brothers and sister that nothing is impossible. I want to show Emily the same thing. I want to prove it to her. With my life, my decisions, my business."

Sydney's gaze flicked from Luke to the baby. The intensity of her blue eyes faded, erasing the shine that had been there before. "But remember, kids don't care so much about how successful their parents or guardians are as much as they simply want to be shown how important they are. They want to be loved.''

Struck by her statement, Luke jerked to his feet. ''You don't think I love my daughter?''

''I didn't say that.'' She took a slow, deliberate breath. ''Luke, I meant that dreams are just that. But kids are reality.''

Adrenaline charged through his veins. His eagerness to share his thoughts dispersed, replaced by agitation. Defensive, he paced the room. ''Why do you think I'm doing all this? Because of Emily. For my daughter. I want to be able to spend time with her. I want to—''

''Luke,'' she interrupted, her voice calmer than his had been, ''you're not understanding what I'm saying.''

The wind yanked from his sails, he plopped back down on the edge of the couch. ''Then explain it to me.''

Sydney turned her chair to face him more fully, but she ducked her head. A shadow crossed her face, hiding her expression. After a moment's pause, she glanced up and her eyes were filled with a deep sadness that he felt ricochet through his heart. ''You wouldn't understand.''

''Try me.''

She remained silent for a long while. The skin along the column of her throat seemed to tighten and stretch with each exaggerated swallow. Her gaze shifted from Emily to Luke, then back. Finally, she said, ''I'm not accusing you.'' Her voice grated with a husky emotion he couldn't name. ''I'm not bashing your dreams or your idea.

''I agree. I think it can work. Maybe there's a better way than what we've come up with so far. I guess I wanted you to understand that on the surface things often look very different than reality.''

Why did he sense she was talking about something completely different? Confused, he shook his head. ''Are you saying you're not going after your own dreams? But you've said—''

''I know what I said.'' She studied her hand, rubbing her thumb across the palm. ''What I still say. I'm just as you described.'' Her voice warbled. ''I'm career-oriented.''

He leaned forward, wanting to reach out, touch her, comfort her, find out what pain she was enduring. But he resisted. He didn't think she'd welcome his gesture. At this point, he knew it wouldn't be a wise move. ''Is it because you have to be?''

Her head jerked up. Her eyes narrowed. It felt as if she'd slammed a door in his face. She'd shut him out. And he felt a cold emptiness inside him. Had he said something wrong?

''What?'' he asked. ''What did I say?''

''Nothing.'' She faced the desk and calculator again. ''Let's get back to work.''

''Wait a minute. I want to know—''

''Drop it.'' She shrugged off his hand. ''It's none of your business.''

A slap to the face couldn't have hurt worse. He cursed himself. Clearing his throat, he pushed down his regret. She was right. It was none of his business. But he cared. He'd hurt her. And he hadn't meant to.

''I didn't mean to insult you,'' he said, haltingly. ''I-I only meant that maybe you were like my mother. She was forced to join the workforce because of her divorce. I thought maybe that's how you felt. Maybe I was wrong.''

Only the soft clicks of her nails against the number keys filled the room. Even Emily remained quiet in her playpen. The silence worked on Luke's nerves, like an emery board chafing, filing, eroding his peace of mind. How had things changed so abruptly? What had he done? What had he said?

As she reworked some of the figures, Sydney said in a voice barely above a whisper, ''You weren't.''

Her statement stunned Luke. It turned the picture he had in his mind of her upside down. It should have scared the stuffing out of him. Usually when he heard a woman recant her career-oriented posture, he took off running. How many women had told him they'd changed their minds? They suddenly wanted a relationship instead of a career. A relationship with him! But Sydney wasn't saying that. She wasn't asking for anything, except maybe a little peace.

He stared at her bent head, wanting to look into her eyes, knowing if he did that he wouldn't be able to resist the tormented look. He wanted to wrap his arms around her, rest her head against his shoulder, take away her pain. But how could he? With a kiss? A date? With...what did he have to offer her?

As she continued working, ignoring him, he realized she didn't want sympathy. She only wanted understanding. All he had to offer her was friendship.

Following her lead, he resisted asking more questions, resisted the urge to comfort her with a hand on her shoulder, a caress against her pale cheek, a brush of his lips against hers. Instead, he shifted the conversation back to a work mode. "It'll take time to figure out my target market. But I believe in this, Sydney. I think it can work. But you're right, there's got to be a better way to accomplish the same thing without costing as much out of pocket."

She skimmed the palms of her hands down her blue jeans. It was the first time he'd seen her dressed casually, without a suit, hose and pumps. He wished the clothes would make her look frumpy or dowdy or something other than just plain sexy. The snug jeans made her legs look forever long. Her crisp white shirt made her hair look like sun-drenched apples on a warm autumn day and accented her pale, opalescent complexion.

He tried to concentrate on the numbers she tallied with the calculator. But his gaze strayed. His mind wandered.

He folded his hands into fists and fought against his attraction.

"I agree," she said, her tone crisp and professional. One finger followed the long line of numbers he'd put together, while the other hand followed the white tape, double checking her keying accuracy. "There's definitely a need out there with single fathers. I think they'll gobble up your products. But first you have to get the catalog in the right hands. That, all by itself, will escalate your costs."

He nodded, wondering why she was here, helping him more than she already had with Emily. Didn't she have a life of her own? Or did she sense, as he did, that a friendship had formed between them? If only he could read her mind. If only...

He stopped himself right there. No. They'd both decided that there could be nothing between them. Physically. Sexually. Emotionally. That was final. But he knew their rationalizations were pure garbage. They'd already crossed the line which seemed blurry and out of focus. There was something there between them, almost palpable. But they were both choosing to ignore it.

"There are address lists," he stated, forcing himself to focus on his future career as well as Sydney concentrated on her own, "I can purchase the ones which will help target the right group. But that doesn't guarantee even one sale."

"Correct. A safe assumption is that you wouldn't make a profit for at least six months. Maybe even the first year." She met his gaze then, her eyes sharp with a professional intensity. "It'll take time for you to break even."

Fixing his thoughts on how much money he might have to dump into this crazy endeavor, he imagined the Cookie Monster he'd shown Emily on television earlier that morning eating his savings as fast as the bite-size cookies the puppet liked to eat.

Emily grunted and lifted her arms toward him. Needing

her sweet distraction from Sydney, he scooped his daughter up into his arms. "Whatcha need, Em?"

She babbled in a nonsensical, musical way. He jiggled her until he received a slobbery smile. That, all by itself, boosted his confidence and his resolve. He couldn't forget why he was doing this—for Emily.

"I guess I can afford a loss at first."

"For a while," Sydney countered.

"True. But—" he voiced his concerns "—the risk seems too high. I'd feel better if I didn't dig such a deep hole."

Sydney ran her fingers through her short-cropped hair. A tuft of red flames stood up along her crown. He found it alluring, intriguing and too damn sexy. He had an urge to smooth it down, but resisted. Instead, he combed Emily's fine, dark hair with his fingers.

Needing distance from Sydney, space for his attraction to cool, so he could contemplate his choices rationally, he paced from one end of the den to the other. Emily gurgled and cooed while tugging at the back of his hair. What was he going to do? He couldn't jeopardize their savings in order to find himself a job. They'd be better off if he kept the money in the bank and simply played house daddy.

But that would drive him crazy. He needed something to challenge him, besides searching for Emily's pacifier. Still, he wanted time to do those things for her. He wanted to help her learn to walk, put a puzzle together, read a book. He wanted it all. Was that too much to ask?

Sydney swiveled her chair around. Her face flushed with excitement, and her eyes sparkled with hope. "What if you turned the catalog into a website? With articles, advice columns, recipes." She emphasized the word that sounded like a cash register. "And, of course, memberships."

They shared a smile. A ray of hope shot through him.

"That would generate revenue right off the bat," he added.

"Exactly. Still, you'll take a hit at the outset, with getting online and the server costs of setting up the website."

In his enthusiasm, he hugged Emily too tight and she squealed a protest. He gave his daughter a loud peck on the cheek. "What d'you think, Em?"

Sydney's smile widened and a dimple pinched her cheek. "You could also have a section with the items you're offering for sale. Like a small catalog within the website."

He hefted Emily above his head and settled her onto his shoulders. "Great idea, Sydney. What would I do without you?" His question vibrated between them.

What had he said? What had he insinuated? That he couldn't live without her? That he needed her? Of course, that was ridiculous. Wasn't it?

Sydney had shown him clearly over the last couple of weeks that he could manage without a mother for Emily, that he was capable of being the kind of father he wanted to be for his daughter. If he could handle this father thing, then he could handle this business, too. Alone.

The honest truth was what stopped him cold. He enjoyed sharing these ideas, these plans with Sydney. He liked trying to solve a problem with her. Frankly, he liked spending time with her, no matter if they were changing diapers, stirring up a batch of brownies or chatting about sunsets and rainstorms.

He knew that was more dangerous than standing out in the middle of a storm holding a lightning rod. It was asking for trouble. Irritated at himself, he shook off his thoughts. It had been a slip of the tongue. Nothing more. Because it could never be more. Even if he wanted Sydney. Even if he needed her. She didn't need him. She didn't want a hand-me-down family. The cold, hard reality pained him.

"I, uh, appreciate your help on this." He wanted to cover his blunder. But how? "You've been great." He was digging himself in deeper. He stood in the middle of the room, holding Emily on his shoulders, unable to move or breathe or find his way out of the maze in his mind. ''I, um—''

''Luke, you don't have to thank me. It's no big deal. I enjoy doing this sort of thing.''

''You're good at it.''

She flushed at his heartfelt words. He felt the air thickening around him, as if the humidity grew denser. ''You've been a big help to me, too.''

''Then we're even.'' His voice sounded rough with a mixture of emotions he barely recognized as regret and longing.

Sydney gave a succinct nod and tapped a pencil eraser against the desk. ''There are more things you should consider, Luke. Once you're established, then you could branch off and have a separate catalog.''

''There's a lot of possibilities. The answer would depend on what's cost effective.'' He wondered if a relationship with Sydney would be worth the price he'd pay, the price Emily might pay. That doused him with a bucket of reality.

''Precisely. You can make that decision later. But now, you'll have a choice down the road.''

He had no choice in the matter of Sydney, he realized with a pang of regret. The decision had already been made. For Emily. And he'd have to live with it. Even if it hurt like a knife slicing through his heart.

''That's great.'' But it didn't sound great. It sounded horrible. A life without Sydney. He rubbed his jaw, knowing he didn't like the idea of letting Sydney out of his life at all. But the time was fast approaching. Soon, her baby shower would come and go. And in one week, Sydney would be gone.

Feeling his throat ache with suppressed emotions, he said, ''The website will allow me some freedom.'' Time with Emily. ''To develop more products. I wouldn't have to have a full catalog from the start.'' Just as he didn't have to have a full life right now. His social life, his love life was on the back burner. At least until Emily was older. Maybe until she was grown. He'd have to take it day by day. He'd judge the situation by his daughter's needs. ''We could try out different products and see how they sell before we launch into a catalog.''

Is that what he'd been doing with past relationships? Trying out different women? Testing to see if they fit into his life? When had he ever compromised to make a relationship work? Even if he did ever decide to take the plunge into matrimonial waters, his intended would probably have to make more compromises. She'd definitely have to want a family, his Emily.

Old doubts resurfaced, taunted him. It was the same old story. Was he more like his dad? Always moving toward greener pastures? Always searching for something more? Requiring what no woman could ever give?

No. He'd uncovered a special something with Sydney. But his parental responsibilities prevented him from pursuing anything else right now.

Or did it?

There was no rule book, nothing that said he couldn't find someone for himself. He'd simply decided that the second Emily had been placed in his arms. But was it unfair to him? To Emily? Confusion clouded his thinking.

''You could also put your cookbook online and for a fee members could download it,'' Sydney said, continuing their conversation.

He lifted his daughter up over his head and waggled her chubby little body like a soaring kite. ''What do you think, Em?''

Smiling from ear to ear, she cooed. ''Da-da! Eeeee!''

His heart flipped completely over. Pulling her down to him, he hugged her close to his heart. Laughing with pure joy, he glanced toward Sydney. He knew he wasn't making a mistake being a daddy first. But sometimes it was a hard call. "Did you hear her?" His throat worked up and down with wonder. These precious moments were worth every sacrifice. "She called me Da-da."

Sydney nodded. She held the end of a pencil against her lips which compressed into a tight line. Tears filled her eyes.

A gulf opened between them, separating them. Luke knew he'd made the right decision. His only choice.

Chapter Eight

"**D**id your dad ever date?" Luke asked.

Sydney nearly choked on her champagne. While celebrating a successful orange soufflé—one that hadn't fallen flat or bubbled up like a parachute—she hadn't expected that particular question. She stared at him for a moment before she found her voice. "What? I mean, why?"

Deep in thought, Luke paced along the length of his kitchen counter. The golden liquid in his glass sloshed against the side. "I don't know." He stopped, turned and looked boldly into her eyes. As if he was troubled, the skin at the corners of his brown eyes pinched. "Yes, I do. I wanted to know how it affected you and your brothers and sister."

Why? The question gonged in her brain, resonating in her heart. Had he decided to date? Was he concerned about how it would affect Emily? The burning question couldn't be ignored. If he did want to date, who was the lucky woman? The butterflies she always felt in her stomach when Luke was around metamorphosed into gigantic killer bees, stinging her with acute awareness.

"You're concerned about Emily?" She felt her throat knot in a tangle of indistinguishable emotions.

"Exactly."

"Are you, um, thinking of d-dating?" Her face grew warm as if she'd suffered a sunburn. She shouldn't have asked. But she had to know. "I mean, you'd said you weren't interested in a relationship." She slanted a curious gaze at him, realized he was watching her closely, and her pulse skipped. "Has that changed?"

Did she care? Yes, unfortunately, she did—too much.

Luke rolled his broad shoulders in a casual shrug that made his starched shirt crinkle. "I'm wondering about the future."

The future. As in—next weekend? Or as in—when Emily turned sixteen?

"Oh." A wash of disappointment wiped out Sydney's overeagerness, which in itself was absurd. It shouldn't matter if he was interested in dating. She *was not*.

Or was she?

That question scared the daylights out of her. She didn't want to pursue the scenarios filling her mind.

Besides, what if he did want to date? What did it matter to her? He probably didn't want to date *her!* He probably had a thick black book stashed someplace with too many names to count, highlighting past fun dates and future prospects. That mental picture gave her ego a painful snap.

The horrifying fact was she didn't want him to date. Not just anybody! She had a particular woman in mind—herself! Her world shook with that sudden realization.

Turning her back on him, and her desires, she ran a finger around the rim of her glass. She could taste the tartness from the champagne on her lips. The timing was all wrong. Why hadn't they met ten years ago? Before she'd married Stan. Before she'd known what it was like to have a daughter. Before she'd learned she couldn't have a baby.

A lump of regret knotted around her windpipe. It was too late for little-girl infatuations or feminine fantasies about finding love and living happily ever after. She'd married and divorced. Love, she'd learned, was painful and disappointing. Life offered no guarantees. She knew her future would be spent all alone. Not because she was doomed. It was her own choice. She wouldn't allow herself to fill her head with empty hopes.

Even if she longed to feel Luke's mouth on hers again, to taste him, to be held in the security of his arms. Never again would she put herself in a situation where she had to confess her inadequacies to a man she loved. She never wanted to see the dismay, pity and contempt she'd seen in Stan's eyes.

Irritated at her own weakness, she tightened her grip on the wineglass, then took a deep breath to calm her nerves, before she snapped, along with the glass stem. She wanted to ask Luke more questions, to delve further into his reasons for his question about her father dating. After all, inquiring minds wanted to know. But she clamped down her more-than-mild curiosity.

"My dad didn't date for a long while," she said, forcing her thoughts to her younger years. "It took him a while to get over my mother. And, of course, he was busy with his work and trying to raise a family on his own. I don't know if he wanted to date then, or didn't care. He simply didn't."

She found it easier to think about the past than to contemplate a future alone…without Luke. When had she started to care for him? Probably from the moment he'd appeared, haggard and helpless at his front door, needing help with his charming baby. Thankfully, their days together were numbered. Then he'd no longer need her. When she wouldn't have an excuse to help her cook. When she wouldn't be tortured by needs and desires she had no use for.

"Occasionally," she added, "in the last ten years, my dad's gone out with a couple of ladies. Maybe to a church dinner or function. Sometimes to a movie. He once took line dancing lessons with a woman friend. But as far as I know, they were just friends."

"So, he's never remarried?" Luke sounded forlorn, almost frustrated, as if she'd somehow told him he couldn't ever date or marry.

"Never." She slid a glance in his direction. Tufts of his dark hair stood on end as if he'd plowed his hands through the thickness. The lines surrounding his mouth and eyes looked as if they'd been carved into his tan skin with a chisel.

"How would you handle it if he had, if he did now?"

Giving herself a moment before she answered, she glanced up at the white ceiling fan, swirling around like her whirlpooling emotions, then met Luke's gaze. His dark eyes seemed to peer into her soul. With a shaky hand, she set the champagne flute on the counter and crossed her arms in front of her. "I don't know how I would have handled it as a young kid. We were all pretty devastated when my mom died. I might have hated the woman. Or I might have liked her for taking over all the responsibility that had been placed on me. I don't know. I would hope that I would have accepted his choice of a wife...if that's what would have made him happy.

"And now?" She shrugged. "I think all of us would like to see Dad find a nice woman and get married. We want him to be happy, too. But, I don't think he can look past my mother's memory. It's still too vivid in his mind and heart for him to see anyone else."

Luke nodded solemnly as if mulling over her answer. He'd admitted to her he hadn't truly loved Emily's mother. So, that wouldn't stop him from making a commitment to someone else. But what would? His fear, she realized. He feared being like his father. But she knew with her whole heart that he wasn't.

"I can tell you my own experience with kids and dating," Sydney said, wanting to help him with his struggles, even though she didn't want to face the fact he quite possibly could go out with someone else, just might ask her to baby-sit Emily.

Slowly, he raised his gaze to meet hers. Expectancy shimmied between them. The concern that had darkened his features seemed to lift, along with one of his eyebrows. "How's that?"

She leaned against the kitchen counter. Behind her, the soufflé they'd sampled remained in the dish, looking like a picture out of *Martha Stewart Living*. "I was still living at home when I met Stan, my ex-husband. My brothers were in middle school and my sister was still in early elementary school."

"And?" he prodded when she paused, unsure exactly how to explain her siblings' behavior.

"Jennie, especially, thought of me more as her mother than as a big sister. When I brought Stan home to meet Dad for the first time, all hell broke loose. It was as if the kids had planned the whole thing. But they couldn't have thought of anything quite so elaborate."

Crossing the kitchen, Luke helped himself to another serving of soufflé. His shoulder brushed hers, causing her to lose her train of thought. She edged out of his way, needing a safe distance. His dark eyes glittered with interest. "What happened?"

"I'm not sure I remember the order. It all happened simultaneously. Jennie threw a royal fit, crying, slamming doors, pouting. And boy, could she pout. She could make the whole neighborhood miserable when she stuck her bottom lip out."

Luke chuckled. "Em will be the same way."

Nodding, she went on, "Paul and Scott had been outside supposedly watering the yard and shrubs. Basically, doing their regular chores. Paul ran inside, hollering at the top of his lungs. He left the door open and our oversized golden retriever barreled through the house, leaving muddy paw prints across the white downstairs carpet and kitchen linoleum.

Luke paused, holding a spoon full of soufflé midway between the dish and his bowl.

"And Scott." She sighed. "Well, he'd climbed up in the old tree house, so he could get a good look at Mandy Wells, the teen idol of the neighborhood. She was sunbathing in her bikini."

Luke winked. "Gotcha. I think I know where this is headed."

"For disaster." Her heart pumped wildly in response to his sexy wink. He had a smile that could have put Mel Gibson to shame. She glanced away, trying to sort through her suddenly scattered thoughts. What had she been saying?

She felt Luke staring at her, waiting, his gaze like a firm caress along her sensitized skin. Her pulse pounded in her ears like a teenage drummer trying to emulate a rock star, out of sync and too loud to concentrate. She lifted her glass for a sip and realized her hand was trembling. The shaking spread to her limbs and belly. With two unsteady hands, she managed to set the glass on the counter again and clasped her hands behind her back. She stared at the tips of her shoes until she remembered where she'd been in the story.

"Scott had this set of binoculars. But a tree branch was in his way. So he leaned too far out of the tree house window to get a better look at good ol' Mandy, and he toppled the tree house over. And he fell—*splat.*"

"I don't think they planned that one," Luke said with a chuckle.

"Probably not. Actually, I don't think the boys cared if I dated or not. They were busy with their own lives by that point. They'd hit the terrible-teen years. And I was too old, too square for them."

"You weren't groovy?" he asked, his smiling eyes making her knees go limp.

"Cooking, cleaning and laundry made Sydney a dull girl, that's for sure." She had to laugh at the image she dug out of her memories like searching through old albums for a particular photo. She'd had dishpan hands at sixteen. She'd spent most afternoons watching television as she ironed clothes. On rainy days, instead of drooling over a teen magazine, she'd entertained her brothers and sister with games and funny stories. It definitely wasn't the picture of a cheerleader or homecoming queen waiting for her entourage of suitors to call.

She wondered how Luke saw her now. As a boring accountant? She smoothed down her A-line skirt and wished she'd brought jeans to wear or something more casual, more accessible, for her after-work cooking lesson with Luke. Maybe she was hiding behind her business facade, like she'd hidden from the traumas of life behind a zillion chores and baby-sitting responsibilities.

Shrugging off her melancholy thoughts, she continued, "It was quite an evening, to say the least. We spent most of it in the emergency room getting Scott stitched back together. Then the rest of the night, I spent on my hands and knees cleaning up after Goldie."

"Goldie?"

"The dog."

"Oh, the paw prints." Luke's smile required sunglasses for closer inspection. "So, you latched onto Stan, thinking you'd never find anyone brave enough to pick you up for a date again?"

Her own smile faded at the thought of her ex-husband.

"No, actually, he was sweet through the whole ordeal. He even helped scrub the kitchen floor."

"That's the man of every girl's dreams."

She rolled her eyes at his sarcasm. "For me, it was a fantasy come true. And a welcome relief. I think that episode pushed me to want to be out on my own."

"Pushed you toward Stan?"

"Maybe."

He spooned a generous bite of soufflé into his mouth and concentrated on the tastes and textures. "This is damn good."

Pleasure warmed her from the inside out. "It'll be a hit at the shower."

Luke nodded and licked the back of his spoon. That sensual movement made her remember the feel of his mouth on hers, how she'd longed to taste more of him, for him to enjoy her like a sumptuous spoonful of soufflé. "What about Jennie? How'd she take your getting married?"

Sydney gave a heavy sigh as she remembered the squabbles, the tug-of-war she'd felt between her feelings of regret and loss and her need to move on with her life. "It wasn't easy. She was extremely upset. At first, Jennie ignored Stan or said ugly things. She even pulled pranks on him."

"I like her already."

Giving a rueful smile, Sydney shook her head. "She was a terror during that period. One time, she booby-trapped the front door, setting a string across the threshold and a bucket of water overhead. I think she saw something similar on the *Brady Bunch*. When Stan walked in one Saturday afternoon, he tripped over the string, which made the water dump on him. It also made the brick entryway incredibly slick."

Luke's brows arched. "And dangerous."

"Exactly. If his hands had been empty, he might have been okay. Then he could have braced himself, caught himself as he fell. Or regained his balance. But he was carrying a cake he'd picked up at the grocery store and flowers for me. He fell flat on his face.'' A wry grin tugged at her mouth and she fought to erase it. "So, we made another trip to the emergency room.''

To her relief, Luke chuckled, then suppressed it. "Sorry. Guess that's not so funny. Was he all right?''

"Once his broken nose healed. Till then he was in a pretty sour mood." She dipped her spoon into the soufflé for an extra bite of the creamy confection. Her brow puckered as she put on her big-sister frown. "I was angry at Jennie, too. But I know she didn't mean for him to get hurt. But now—'' she felt the pull at the corner of her mouth "—it is kind of funny.''

"Kind of?" Luke asked, his smile widening.

Sydney joined in his laughter. The giddy feeling made her feel lighter than the soufflé, free of responsibilities, free from the bondage of her past marriage.

"I played a few tricks of my own," Luke said, battling his own mischievous smile. If he'd been wearing a baseball cap, Luke would have reminded her of one of her brothers. A warmth of affectionate memories flooded her.

"On whom?" she asked, feeling close to Luke, as if a string of understanding connected their hearts.

"My dad's girlfriends. And he had a lot of them. I liked to think at one time that they didn't last long because I scared them away. But now I know that my dad just liked a smorgasbord.''

She caught the subtle change in his dark eyes, and knew instantly, in spite of his lighter tone, that his mood had plummeted down a steep embankment of jagged-edged emotions. Her smile faded like the light at the end of the day and sympathy darkened her heart. "Was that hard on you?''

Again, he shrugged, as if his shirt didn't fit right. He

ducked his head and twisted a dish towel between his hands. "I didn't see him a whole lot. Which was fine by me. When I did, there always seemed to be a new woman in his life. I hated all of them. Because I wanted my dad to come back to my mom and me. But he didn't. He wouldn't have ever done that. And now, I'm glad he didn't."

She understood then he'd asked about her family, because looking into his own past was too painful. Sensing a deep wound in Luke, one that made him edgy and uncomfortable, she eased the subject away from his dad. "Did your mom date much?"

"Every now and then. When she did, I acted very protective of her. I was what you might call obnoxious." He took a gulp of champagne and leaned his elbows on the counter. "How did you handle Jennie's problem, her resentment of Stan?"

Remembering the tears, the fights, Sydney smiled ruefully. "She was a handful. For the next few months, I made sure I set aside time each day for her. Sometimes we played *Clue*, which was her favorite game of all time. Or we went shopping. Or sometimes, we'd close my bedroom door, crawl up on the bed and munch on popcorn and giggle. It didn't have to be elaborate or expensive. She simply wanted me to spend time with her, to keep reminding her that she was important to me."

"That's the key then."

"Precisely. If and when you choose to date..." she couldn't look him in the eye when she mentioned his dating for fear he might read more into her than she cared to let him see "...make sure Emily knows you love her and feels secure. Keep those lines of communication open."

"Of course that might not be a problem, if I started dating right away...while she's still a baby."

Sydney nodded and swallowed the sudden lump in her

throat. "Sure. Then your dating would be a way of life for her. Something she's always known. But—"

His right eyebrow lifted in question. "What?"

"There will be times, even if Emily is used to you dating, when she'll act selfish about her time with you."

He bristled. "I'm not going to sacrifice my relationship with my daughter. I won't take away anything from her. I-I...I simply wanted to add to her world. Maybe."

He moved away from Sydney, pacing in the middle of the kitchen. His breathing sounded sharp and labored.

"Add a mother, you mean?"

"Maybe. I always wanted a brother or sister. I didn't care which. I thought it would be wonderful to have someone to play with, to share things with. I wanted a complete family. You're very lucky to have your siblings."

Sometimes she didn't feel so lucky. But she knew what Luke was getting at. He wanted that for Emily. He wanted the whole package—wife, kids. Things she couldn't give him or Emily. Her heart ached with the raw longings she'd tried so hard to repress.

"Do you see them often, now that you all live in the same city?"

Sydney felt as if he'd punched her in the stomach. Her heart twisted with regrets. "Jennie's a college student. And the boys, well, they're busy establishing their careers."

He tilted his head, as if confused by her statement, and studied her more closely. Her insides shifted uncomfortably. "Didn't you move here to be closer to them?"

"I'm here if they need me." She felt the probing truth of his question deep in her heart. "But, like you said, they're grown. They have their own lives." She shifted uneasily from foot to foot. "In a lot of ways, that part of my life is over. They don't need me like they used to."

Sympathy made his eyes look as soft and mushy as dark, melted chocolate. "That must be hard—"

"Luke." She cut him off. Hot tears burned the backs of her eyes. Feeling herself begin to unravel, she gripped her arms, trying to hold herself together. She swallowed hard and the muscles in her throat tightened. The best defense was a good offense. She had to get his focus off her. So, she spoke the words she'd hidden in her heart. "I know you think you're like your own father. Reckless. A lady-killer. I know he caused you and your mother a lot of hurt and anguish.

"But don't worry about dating. If you meet someone you like, then go for it." The words tasted like bile in her mouth. It was best, she decided, if he dated other women...anyone other than herself. "Don't fall for the line you keep feeding yourself, that you're like your father. You're not. If you were, then you wouldn't be so concerned about Emily.

"I've never seen a sweeter, more caring father than you have been for your daughter." She choked on tears. A myriad of scenes spun around her head of Luke kissing Emily, changing a diaper, playing patty cake. Those large hands clapping against Emily's short, stubby hands made her chest ache.

He was a good father. He didn't need her help anymore.

He'd make an adoring husband. For some other woman! Not her. He didn't need a barren wife. He needed someone who could give him more children...and Emily brothers and sisters.

Once again, she felt lost, without a purpose. Her siblings didn't need her. Luke didn't either. She was all alone.

Needing to escape, needing to spend time alone to sort through her thoughts, and get her longings under control, Sydney took a step forward and grasped Luke's arm. Then raising up on tiptoes she kissed him on the cheek. She wanted him to understand her words came from the heart.

She needed to say goodbye before this quicksand of desire and longings swallowed her whole.

The hard plane of his face felt warm and rough against her lips, like a tree trunk heated by the summer sun. She thought of lovers carving their initials in wood, proclaiming their love, and her heart missed a beat. Abruptly, she pulled away from him and reached for her purse to leave. She couldn't stay any longer. She felt her heart pounding, pounding for release against the bonds she'd placed around it. The chains were for her protection, from the hopes and dreams she'd harbored, from a lover's rejection when he learned the truth.

Luke grabbed her wrist and pulled her back to him. Her breasts met his chest squarely. She felt his tough leanness. She felt his overwhelming warmth as his arms came around her and held her tight. The tension pulsed between them as he stared into her eyes, then flicked his gaze across her aching lips. She wanted him. Body, heart and soul. And she needed this kiss like she needed air to breathe. This one last kiss.

But he waited, took his sweet, unnerving time. His hand cupped her chin, caressed her jaw. Ripples of awareness undulated through her. His touch felt lazy, erotic, yet felt as if he suddenly possessed her.

"Say no if you don't want this as much as I do." His voice sounded raspy, hoarse with raw emotions that reverberated inside her.

It would be her undoing. Fear seized her. How would she cope with those needs and desires again? How would she stuff them inside her heart once they'd been set free?

"No." She mouthed the word. Fear made her try to resist. She knew his kiss would release her longings with one simple touch. But her need silenced her own protest.

With a barely noticeable shake of his head, Luke placed his mouth over hers. In that moment, he stole her breath and her ability to think. A sigh expanded her chest, as she felt herself falling…falling into him. Where she found the sheltering place she'd been searching for her entire life.

She opened to him, and he deftly explored every crevice, nuance and pleasure within her with his tongue and lips. His hands moved over her in sensuous caresses that ignited a burst of flames inside her. She felt herself consumed with longing.

But could those desires ever be fulfilled?

The resonating question doused her with a cold bucket of reality.

Chapter Nine

All alone, Luke stood in his kitchen, shocked, transfixed, aching. He could still smell Sydney's tempting fragrance. Her scent clung to his hands, his shirt and his whirling senses. Disoriented at how something so right could have turned into something so wrong, he slumped against the counter.

He'd kissed her, even though she'd said in less than a whisper that she didn't want it…or him. He'd known better. He'd seen the longing in her eyes, recognized it easily, because it mirrored his own desires. He wanted Sydney not only as a man aches for a woman, but also as a soul longs for a mate.

He'd never thought of marriage, never contemplated it, not even when Sheila had shown up on his doorstep carrying Emily. After all, he'd told himself he wasn't capable of being a good husband or a father. He'd never wanted to hurt anyone, as his father had hurt his mother…and him.

But now, for some insane reason, he wanted the chance to prove his own theory wrong. He wanted to be a wonderful father to Emily. He wanted to be a great husband to... To Sydney?

Somehow, it felt like the most natural progression. Trouble was, he wasn't sure Sydney would feel the same way. Or that she wanted another secondhand family. That cut a slice out of his heart.

He and Emily were a pair. They went together. They had to be accepted as a whole in any relationship. He didn't think his daughter would suffer if he dated or eventually married Sydney. In fact, she'd benefit. She'd be able to observe a loving couple, which he'd never experienced. She'd learn what honor, trust and love were all about. She'd understand commitment meant security rather than something to be feared or scorned.

Because Sydney had started teaching Luke the same things.

She'd taught him the meaning of selfless devotion, of giving oneself to loved ones. Obligation and responsibility weren't ugly three-dollar words. They had meaning. They had honor. Sydney had helped him see the seeds within himself. He knew with her by his side they could be nourished to grow and flourish.

A staccato cry echoed through the house. His senses went on full alert. Automatically, without hesitation, he headed toward Emily's room.

The hall light cast a soft glow into the nursery. Shadows loitered in the corners, behind the rocker, under the crib. Emily stood in her Winnie-the-Pooh pajamas, gripping the rails. She lifted one foot, then the other, as if trying to figure out a way to climb out of the crib. Her diaper crinkled with each frustrated stamp. Her face turned red as a beet. Tears streamed down her pudgy cheeks. Her wails pierced his eardrums and tattooed his heart with agony only a father could know.

He scooped her into his arms. Her soft, warm body cuddled against him and assured him she was fine. His heart swelled to overflowing with love. Even with only a few weeks of fatherhood under his belt, he had a hard time remembering life without Emily. Or even without Sydney.

He tried to shush his daughter's tears. "It's okay now, Em. Daddy's here. I won't let anything hurt you."

Jiggling her against his shoulder, he felt her tears dampen his shirt. She smelled sugary sweet, like honey and lollipops, a combination that made him smile. He rocked from side to side. "You're okay, honey. You're safe with Daddy."

Holding his daughter, snuggling her close, he realized that all he'd ever wanted was a family. It hadn't been a conscious desire or a spoken wish. But he realized then, that's why Sydney made him feel complete. She finished their family circle. He needed her. Not to do laundry or cook and clean. Not even to raise his child. That was a job he wanted. He simply needed Sydney's smile, her understanding, her love.

But she didn't want the package.

And he couldn't settle for less.

What had she done?

As Sydney pulled into her driveway thirty minutes after leaving Luke's house, she knew it had been a reckless mistake. She'd kissed Luke. She could still feel his mouth moving over hers in the slowest, most erotic way she'd ever experienced. She'd kissed him back with all the pent-up passion she held inside her frustrated body. Kissed him like there would be no tomorrow. Kissed him like she'd meant it.

Had she?

Maybe, she thought, with a pang of regret. But there wasn't a future for them.

Why? Why, oh why, had she done such a foolish thing?

That answer came too easily in the frantic beating of her heart. She wanted Luke. More than she'd wanted any man. Needed him, like she'd never needed anyone before.

She'd raised herself not to depend on others. After her mother had died, she hadn't relied on her daddy. She'd struggled through, carrying too many burdens on her own. As a married woman, she'd pursued her college degree, too much of a realist to believe Stan would always be there to take care of her, to protect her. And he hadn't. At the first sign of hardship, he'd run into another woman's arms. She'd closed up her heart and locked away her dreams as unrealistic fantasies.

But Luke had wrenched open her heart, shone a light on the cobwebs inside her soul. She needed him. And it scared the stuffing out of her.

Clutching the steering wheel as if it might turn the car around and take her right back to Luke, she knew it was more than the physical attraction ricocheting between them, like tennis pros volleying at the net. They'd connected. They'd enjoyed frolicking evenings along with warm, romantic sunsets. But there was more. Much more. They'd shared their hearts, their souls, their hurts and pains, their heartaches and heartbreaks.

Well, at least Luke had. She'd kept a dark secret inside her like a prisoner of war. She wouldn't...*couldn't,* let it out for fear of Luke's reaction. For fear it would be her undoing.

She'd seen the pure joy on his face when he held his tiny, precious daughter, and the sizzling desire when he'd looked at Sydney. What hurt most was the memory of him telling Emily that he wanted to give her siblings. Sydney couldn't forget that moment. She knew she couldn't be that woman.

A fracture rent her heart in two, the jagged edges ripping and tearing at her soul. In that instant, she knew she was toppling head over heels in love with Luke Crandall. Despair sucked her into its depths and swallowed her whole.

As she spun in the blaring red vortex of anguish, she wondered how she'd found the resistance to leave him, to push him away, to escape the love waiting for her in his house? Only one answer occurred to her. It held the resonating truth. Fear.

She feared what he would say when she told him the truth. She feared what he would do. Would he reject her, as Stan had? Would he pity her?

She couldn't have survived that. Fear had propelled her home, out of his arms, away from his tempting kisses. She wrapped her arms around herself, feeling a shiver shudder through her, and knew she couldn't ever take that risk and tell Luke she was barren. She felt the aching emptiness deep inside her soul.

Luke rocked Emily until he thought his arms would fall out of their sockets. He sang her favorite song until his throat felt raw. He finally moved to the den and paced, holding his sniffling, hiccuping, unhappy daughter against his shoulder.

What was wrong? She'd been difficult to put down before, but never this hard. Over the last few weeks, with Sydney working with him, Emily had settled into a schedule of sleeping most of the night. Every now and then, she woke and he'd patted her until she'd been pacified.

But not tonight.

Tonight, when he wanted to wallow in regret over Sydney, figure out how to wrangle her into their lives permanently, Emily wouldn't allow him the luxury of even five minutes alone or one minute of silence. Every time he tried to place her back in the crib she started to cry. If he left her anyway, hoping she'd settle down on her own, her tears became wails of despair shredding his peace of mind, ripping apart his heart.

What on earth was the matter with his baby? Did she sense his pain, his frustration, his desperation? Or was she sick? Did she have an upset tummy? A fever?

For the fiftieth time, he felt her warm, clammy forehead. How could he tell if she had a fever? She always felt like a little oven to him. With her face reddened by her agitated cries, she felt downright hot.

Concern wrinkled his brow. He paced along the windows in the den, bouncing Emily in his arms, murmuring to her. His nerves were shattered. Emily had exhausted his patience, her cries jumbling his composure.

As the minutes passed in slow progression toward midnight, then marched on toward dawn, exhaustion settled into his bones and frustration wrenched away his control. Desperate for help, he reached for the phone to call the one person who could help him through this crisis which seemed epic in proportions.

"Hello?" Her voice sounded groggy, husky with sleep, and as sexy as Demi Moore's.

"Sydney?"

"Luke?" Her voice jerked as if she'd sat up in bed. He heard the rustle of sheets, and wondered if it was the sound of cotton sheets chafing her silken nightgown. "What time is it?"

He pictured her brushing her auburn hair out of her blue eyes. "Late...early. About three."

Emily snuffled against his shoulder and he patted her backside with his cupped hand. Had he done the right thing? Or should he have gritted his teeth and lost a night's sleep? He heard the silence on Sydney's end of the phone. Had she fallen back to sleep? Was she irritated? His stomach twisted in a pretzel-shaped knot.

"Something's wrong with Emily," he said, his voice cracking.

There was a heartbeat of a hesitation before she asked, "Where are you?"

"Home."

"I'll be right over."

No "call a doctor," or "what's the matter this time?" Grateful for her understanding, her graciousness, her concern, he settled the phone in the receiver and waited for Sydney.

When Sydney walked into Luke's house, Emily's tears dried and she clapped her hands with glee. With a rueful smile, Sydney shook her head and said, "You little faker. There's nothing wrong with you, is there?"

"She's been crying nonstop since about ten-thirty." Luke's voice sounded as if it had been through a shredder. He looked frazzled, like a bird who'd been in a fight, his feathers all ruffled and standing out in disarray. His eyes were red with deep circles beneath them, giving him a hawkish look.

Sydney's heart twisted. Sympathy urged her to put her arms around him. Using every ounce of resistance, she stopped herself from rushing forward. Instead, she slipped off her tennis shoes, to prove she wouldn't bolt for the door.

"Here." She reached for Emily and hefted the baby into her arms. Emily wrapped her arms and legs around Sydney and snuggled close. "Give yourself a break, Luke. Let me see if I can get her to go back to sleep."

"Thanks, Sydney. You can't know how I appreciate this."

"Don't worry about it. I'm glad you called." She walked down the dimly lit hallway toward Emily's bedroom, her socked feet shuffling across the carpet. Luke matched her step for step. With only a foot or so separating them, she felt his virile presence like a warm blanket wrapped around her. His breath caressed her cheek and her stomach dropped. When he reached out and grasped his daughter's hand, he brushed his fingers against Sydney's back and a ripple of anticipation undulated down her spine. The setting seemed too intimate for her to keep her wits about her.

"When did you last change her?" she asked, trying to keep her focus on the baby.

"Thirty minutes ago."

"Did you feed her?"

"About eleven."

"Hmm. What's wrong, li'l one? Why aren't you as tired as your daddy?"

Emily waved her arms in the air. "Da-da-da-da-da!"

Sydney shifted the little girl in her arms, cradling her in the crook of her arm. "It's time for bed now." She settled into the rocker. "Let's see if we can't make you sleepy."

"I tried that," Luke said, watching intently.

"You know—" Sydney wiped drool off Emily's chin with a cotton diaper "—she might be teething. Why don't you get that medicine from her bag? I'll put some on her gums."

He nodded and found the diaper bag.

A few minutes later, Sydney smoothed the cream onto Emily's gums. The baby started to fuss and cry. She tried to wiggle out of Sydney's grasp.

"Her gums are sore. I think she's got a tooth trying to come in. Has she been drooling a lot lately?"

"What do you mean by a lot?"

"More than usual."

"I don't know. I haven't measured it. It's always seemed like a lot to me."

"Well, it can be a sign."

"Oh."

Sydney settled back in the rocker. "Let's give this a chance to work."

Luke stared down at them as if holding his breath, waiting for Emily to suddenly fall back to sleep. The shadows in the room made his profile dark and ruggedly handsome. His gaze held a soft, intimate glow, like the light from a fire. Her insides shifted nervously.

"Luke," Sydney whispered, "why don't you go in the den and get some rest? We'll be fine."

"What if you need me?"

"Then you'll hear Emily crying. Trust me," she said, hoping he did, wanting him to, needing him to feel comfortable with her taking charge of his daughter. "We're fine."

Slowly, he nodded. But he seemed reluctant to leave. He took a hesitant step backward. "You're sure?"

"Yes. Go."

Before he left, he smoothed a knuckle along Emily's brow, then settled his hand on Sydney's shoulder. He gave her a slight squeeze. His eyes bored into her with a solid heat that made her shiver. "Thanks."

He backed out of the room and left them alone with only the whir of the ceiling fan for company.

An hour later, Sydney rocked a sleeping Emily and felt her own eyes droop closed. The darkness made her feel as if she floated on shadowy clouds. The baby's warmth nestled into her heart. Curled into a tiny fist, Emily's little hand rested limply against Sydney's shoulder, offering her trust and acceptance. If only for this one moment, this baby needed Sydney. She handed over her trust and acceptance. It brought the same heady feeling as when Luke had called for help.

Then a steady, firm hand on her shoulder made her eyelids pop open with surprise. Her heart jolted. Her pulse quickened as her vision came into focus. She stared into Luke's smiling face.

"You fell asleep," he said in a husky whisper that caused a tingling in the pit of her stomach.

She swallowed but couldn't manage an answer. She stared at him as if dumbstruck. The silence stretched between them like a rubber toy.

"Want me to put her down?" he asked, already scooping his daughter into his arms.

His arm brushed her middle, his hand skimmed along the underside of her breast in a cautious attempt not to wake his daughter. Sydney thought the quaking in her limbs would have woken the whole city. Amazingly, he straightened, inching away from Sydney, and held Emily against him like a sack of potatoes. The baby never woke.

Sydney couldn't find the strength to stand. She watched Luke settle his baby into her crib with gentleness and concern. She felt her heart swelling with each beat. Tenderly, Luke covered his sleeping daughter with a pink blanket. Then he turned to face Sydney.

Her heart kicked into gear. She'd never felt so awake in her life, so alive with each vibrating sensation that pulsed through her.

He held out his hand to her. "Come on."

Slowly, cautiously, she placed her hand in his. Awareness ricocheted through her body. Still, his easy smile remained intact when she thought her heart might burst out of her chest. As he helped her to her tired feet, he didn't move away and give her more space. He remained only a breath away. His gaze darkened to midnight, softening with a glow that reminded her of a full moon. He touched her cheek with a featherlike caress. "You're tired. Why don't you sleep in my bed till morning?"

"B-but—" Her heart jackhammered its way into her throat.

His smile widened. "I'll stay on the couch."

"I don't know. I should probably go on home."

"It's too dangerous. I don't want you driving when you're this tired." He intertwined his fingers with hers and clasped her hand tightly, then he dipped his head and brushed a tender kiss across her lips. Her common sense buckled. "Thanks for your help."

"Any time." And she meant it.

His mouth curved in an enticing way that made her want to kiss him again. Her insides rippled, and her skin tightened with desire.

"Come on. I'll tuck you in bed." The seduction in his voice made her insides curl with anticipation.

Sydney crawled into Luke's king-size bed, too aware of him to notice his bedroom, too tired to pull him down with her. He stuck to his word and tucked her safely beneath the covers, planted a soft kiss of promise on her forehead and wished her a good night's sleep.

She'd thought she wouldn't sleep a wink after that.

But she slept soundly.

And her dreams had revolved around Luke.

She dreamed of him kissing her, and her kissing him. Of his mouth, whispering words of love and eliciting shock waves from her body. Of his hands, soft and gentle and skillful, moving over her body, exploring, uncovering hidden secrets.

She sat bolt upright in bed and blinked twice. A sliver of light slanted through the blinds, and she knew morning had arrived. She pushed a lock of hair off her sweaty forehead. What was she doing in Luke's bed?

With her heart battering her breastbone, she scrambled out of his four-poster bed, pushing aside the warmed sheets and comforter. She ran a shaky hand down her wrinkled clothes. Where were her shoes? Oh, yes, by the front door. She finger-combed her hair and tried to straighten the covers on the bed, tried to erase any traces that she'd been there, and noticed only one head-dent in a pillow. The other pillow remained smooth and untouched. So, she'd slept alone, with Luke holding her only in her dreams. Is that how it would always be?

Yes. That's how it had to be.

Cautiously, she edged toward the door and listened intently to the silence filling the house. She glanced at her wrist watch and realized it was almost seven. She needed to go home and shower for work.

Slipping into the hallway, she tiptoed past a couple of closed doors. Outside Emily's nursery, she heard a rustling, the familiar crinkling of a diaper. She peeked into the room, and Emily smiled. Cooing softly, the baby crawled to one end of the crib and pushed herself to her wobbly feet. She looked over the rails at Sydney imploringly.

"Okay," she mumbled, unable to resist the baby's silent request and her own irrepressible needs. She lifted the baby into her arms and couldn't hold back her own smile. She loved the soft smells of morning clinging to the baby's pajamas. Smoothing back the baby-fine hair, she kissed the little girl's warm forehead. "Morning, Emily. How are you feeling today?"

The baby rocked, kicking her legs and waving her arms.

"I bet you're hungry. Let's go see if we can't find you a bottle." She caught a little fist and gave it a playful kiss.

She carried the baby through the den. It was still dark, the drapes closed. When she saw Luke sprawled on the sofa, she paused. Even through the dimness, she made out his form. He looked peaceful, his hair tousled, the lines on his face relaxed. He slept soundly with one arm slung above his head. His feet hung off the end of the sofa. A pulse of desire beat chaotically at the base of her throat.

She wanted to touch him, to stir him awake with a surprise kiss. But she didn't dare. She shouldn't wake him.

He'd insist on taking care of his daughter. And he probably needed his sleep.

Carefully, she moved past him toward the kitchen. Emily gurgled. Sydney pressed a finger to the little girl's lips. "Shh. Daddy's sleeping."

Emily tried to bite Sydney's finger, and she tickled the baby's sides, wringing another smile out of her. As she reached the kitchen, she paused. The light from the windows washed the breakfast nook in a pale glow that shimmered against a vertical row of plaques on the wall. Curious, she moved closer.

"Are these your daddy's?" she whispered, reading Luke's name etched in brass.

Squinting in the pale light, she read first one, then another and another. Her eyes widened with each prize. Her breath caught in her throat as comprehension dawned.

"Oh, my God."

"What's this?" Sydney jabbed Luke's foot with the point of a wooden plaque. Anger rolled through her, crushing her hope, crumbling her trust in Luke's abilities.

He grunted, shifted on the sofa then rubbed at his eyes. "Oh, Sydney. Are you awake already?" His gaze drifted over her in a lazy manner that only chafed her anger even more. He gave his daughter a smile that beat all smiles. "Hi, honeybun! I didn't hear you stir."

Emily waggled her arms in response.

"Have you been up with her long, Sydney?" he asked, pushing up on his elbows. "Time for breakfast?"

"Time for you to explain a few things," Sydney said, her voice cold, her blood like ice.

Luke froze. He stared at her, obviously perplexed, his brows coming together at a point above the bridge of his nose. "Did I miss something?"

"No, I did. I accepted your word." She laughed, a caustic sound that mirrored her mood. "I even bought what Roxie said about you."

"Which was?"

She tossed him his precious award and felt the confidence she'd gained in the kitchen over the last few weeks disintegrate. She'd believed in Luke's abilities. But it was all a sham, all a charade. Just as her marriage had once been. For some reason, this hurt as much, if not more. "You lied. For starters."

He blanched at her words while juggling the award in his hands. Looking down at the engraved plaque, he slowly swung his legs over the side of the sofa and stood. A wry smile tilted one corner of his mouth, but Sydney resisted her attraction easily this time.

"This beer award is very prestigious."

Sydney held Emily against her like a buffer. Otherwise she might have been tempted to wallop the baby's daddy. "I don't care if it's the equivalent of an Oscar. Why didn't you just tell me you weren't qualified to make fancy desserts?"

"Who says I'm not qualified?" he argued.

"That." She pointed to the plaque he held and then to the others on the wall. "You know all about chili and beer! But not much about soufflés." She hoisted Emily higher in her arms. The baby's weight made her back ache. "What did the awards say? Fire brand chili? Gut-bustin' beer! You think you're qualified to make crème brûlée? Well, I don't!"

She pushed Emily toward him, and he took his daughter into his arms, shifting her to his hip. "You lied so I'd help you take care of your baby." She narrowed her gaze on him. Anger burned inside her like one of her well-done batches of baklava. "That was a cheap trick."

Turning on her heel, she headed for the door. Three days remained before the shower. She had a million things to do. Wasting time here, with Luke, was not on her list. Once again, there was no one she could lean on, depend on. This shower was up to her. She'd have to do it all by herself.

"Sydney!" He traipsed after her. "Wait! Let's talk about this."

"There's nothing to talk about. I have three days to get ready for a shower that's going to be a disaster." She gave a bitter laugh. "I guess it'll prove one thing to my boss and her boss and the vice president of the company—that I can't handle responsibility, that I can't come through in a crunch, that I can't even manage a simple little baby shower."

Okay, that was three things, two more ways this shower would destroy her. She felt tears burn the back of her throat. All her hopes and dreams of being promoted began to vanish into thin air, like a puff of smoke.

"That's bull…" Luke stopped himself with a look toward his daughter. Setting Emily in her playpen, he handed his daughter her lamb and stalked back toward Sydney.

She expected anger or fury; after all, she'd stomped on his culinary ego. Instead, his brow was lined with worry and concern. His dark eyes seemed brooding. Sydney stood her ground, but felt her pulse skittering and her mind racing with all she had to do to prepare for the shower.

"These awards, Sydney," he said in a calm voice that sounded as if he were trying to talk her off a ledge, "are my specialties. I don't deny that. But you have to admit we've managed just fine. We've made some wonderful, succulent desserts over the past few weeks."

"Great. You, an expert at chili and beer, and me…an expert at peanut butter and jelly! We're going to make baklava and crème brûlée for my boss…for my boss's boss…for the company's V.P." Her knees gave way with the pressure. She sank to a chair and buried her hands in her hair. What a mess! Her heart stopped. "We're some team, all right."

"We are."

With disbelief, she shook her head. "How will I make all of this stuff? What if the soufflé falls? What if the baklava turns out like... Oh God!" She groaned.

"Sydney, it'll be fine." He knelt beside her, placed a hand on her knee. Her blood pumped hot and fierce. She blamed it on her anger, her frustration, her impending humiliation. She wanted to slap his hand away and at the same time she wanted to cling to it like a lifeline...a lifeline to her heart.

"There are so many things that could go wrong." She felt like having one of her sister's infamous temper tantrums. But what would it solve? She'd still be in a pickle. "There's a lot riding on this shower."

"I know. A move up the corporate ladder."

"Yes. I don't know if a generous helping of crème brûlée with the right consistency and the perfect caramelized topping can help or not. But it certainly can't hurt. A disaster sure won't give me much of a push up that ladder."

"Syd—"

"I know. I know. My work has to merit the promotion. It does." She met his gaze boldly, honestly. But her confidence felt like a deflated balloon at the moment. Dipping her chin, she shook her head with utter defeat. "This could ruin everything I've worked so hard for."

He cupped her chin and forced her to meet his steady gaze. "You're right, Sydney. I was wrong to deceive you. I appreciate all you've done for Emily and me. But don't worry. It'll be okay. I promise. I won't let you fail."

Her heart pounded out a beat of disbelief. His hand felt strong and powerful, as if he could wrestle a miracle or two out of God. Oh, how she wanted to believe. Staring into

Luke's dark, hooded gaze, her heart pounding, she wanted to believe. But she couldn't. He'd misled her. He'd lied.

How could she believe Luke, now, when he said he believed they could make these desserts and put on a successful shower? What if it was only another charade for this man to get what he wanted? But what did Luke want? More help? What?

Unfortunately, she knew this shower meant more to her than it should. She'd wanted to prove to herself it didn't hurt as much as it did to give a baby shower for a friend. She'd wanted to prove herself as a woman, capable of baking and cooking and doing all the things a woman should be able to do, even if she lacked the ability to have children. She'd wanted to prove to her superiors that she was willing to go the extra mile for work, for her career. But this disaster-about-to-happen would only prove her incompetence.

It was hard to own up to the ugly truth behind her reasons for giving Roxie the shower. It made her feel small, petty, self-centered. She'd thought giving this shower was a step on her way to getting on with her life. But maybe it had simply been another step backward.

Her anger gave way to despair. "Luke, why didn't you tell me the truth? Now you've ruined everything!"

"I'm sorry, Sydney. I truly am. I knew I could handle what you needed. But you didn't. I was so desperate. I needed you...your help.

"I thought if you knew the truth, that I'd won these types of awards and that I owned a brew-pub, that you wouldn't believe in me, wouldn't trust me." His dark eyes smoldered with a need...a need that matched her own. "Trust me this once. I won't let you down."

"How can you promise that?" Her voice sounded raspy with raw emotions. "How can I pull this off? I can't. I can't do it all." Tears stung the backs of her eyes. "I can't cook and serve everybody. I can't..." She clamped her jaw shut. She wouldn't confess all her failings. "You know all thirty have responded that they'll be there. Thirty!"

His right eyebrow lifted a notch. "Why don't you call your ever-helpful sister that you said could baby-sit for me? She could help you serve."

His statement twisted her heart with another pinch of reality. "She's too busy."

"What about your brothers? They live in town."

She felt that blow in her stomach. "They've got their own lives, too."

"So you're all alone?"

Her spine stiffened. Abruptly, she stood, but her knees wobbled. "I'll be fine."

"Sydney." He caught her wrist with his hand. Burning tingles erupted along her skin. "We'll replicate those desserts. It'll all work out. Trust me."

The words she'd said to him last night came back to haunt her. He'd trusted her with the care of his daughter. Could she trust him with this? Her future? Her hopes and dreams?

"We?" she said, more as a squeak than an actual word.

"Yes, *we*." He slid his hands up her arms and held her tightly. His warm breath fanned her face and a fire inside her. Even though her insides trembled with uncertainty, she had no choice but to meet his steady, confident gaze.

"We're in this together," he said, his voice sound and full of conviction. "Hell, you drove over in the middle of the night to help me. I won't let you do this party alone. I'll be there. And if we need more help, then I'll call in the Marines."

An ache to lean into him seized her, but she withheld. She needed space. She needed air. A nervous laugh bubbled up inside her. "The Marines? You think they could help?"

"Probably not. But I have friends. I'll call in favors. Whatever it takes."

She had no choice. She had to trust him. Or fail on her own. Either way, she still might end up with mud on her face.

Luke held Emily in his arms and watched Sydney pull out of his driveway. He'd hated to let her go. He'd wanted to hold her, comfort her, reassure her that all of this would work out. But he sensed that words were empty. Sydney needed actions. Well, dammit, he'd show her. He'd prove it to her.

No matter the cost. No matter what it took. Her party would be a success. That would be his gift to her.

She'd hesitantly placed her fragile trust in his hands. Even though she was backed into a corner, she was depending on him. Who had ever depended on him? Emily had been the first in so long, the first he'd allowed to depend on him since his mother. But Sydney had shown him he could be a reliable, competent father. Now, he had to prove to himself and Sydney that she hadn't been wrong.

Chapter Ten

Sydney had wakened at dawn, as if it were the day of her own execution. It very might well be, she thought, with a sour frown. She hadn't slept well since she'd left Luke's house two days ago. Now, here she was sidestepping him in her too-tiny kitchen. Not wanting to depend on him, yet doing it anyway. Not wanting to feel her world turned inside out each time she looked into his smiling brown eyes, but she did feel jumbled and disoriented as if her stomach was parachuting without her.

Traipsing back to the dining room table, she smoothed her hand over her mother's beautiful white linen tablecloth. Beneath her fingers, she felt the embroidered roses as surely as she sensed Luke's presence when he entered the room behind her. With his gaze on her, her skimpy T-shirt suddenly felt too tight, the air as thin as on the top of a mountain and her pulse skittering as if she were about to leap off a cliff.

"It looks great," he said, his voice filled with warmth and admiration. "I'm impressed you did all this yourself."

"It was nothing." She lifted a shoulder in a casual shrug, then wrapped her arms around her middle, holding herself together. The imminent party hadn't stolen her poise. Luke had.

"Looks like all these decorations took you forever to make."

"Not forever. Just a few nights." Without much sleep.

She'd saved money by making bows to decorate the table and arranging flowers for a centerpiece. The sweet scent of roses filled the room with anticipation. The blue-and-pink plastic diaper pins, pacifiers, plastic bottles and rattles added a nice touch as they dangled from ribbons around the vase. Along with her mother's cut-glass punch bowl, she'd set out crystal plates and cups. The baroque silver tray gleamed with fresh polish in the sunlight. She had to admit she was pleased.

"Roxie's a lucky mother-to-be," Luke said.

Sydney's heart pinched, and she had to look away from the table and decorations. How many times had she wanted a baby shower, wanted to feel a baby moving inside her, wanted to hold her own child?

"You okay?" Luke's voice sounded too close and unnerving.

"Sure. Fine." She avoided his steady, probing gaze. Sniffing daintily, she put those fantasies out of her mind. But they remained forever buried in her heart. "How's the baklava?"

"It's ready. Where do you want it?"

"There's another silver tray in the kitchen and a stack of doilies next to it."

"Gotcha." He pointed to his watch. "I've got everything under control here." She noticed the dish towel slung over his shoulder. The flowery pattern emphasized his strength and virility. Her insides tingled. "Why don't you go get ready?"

"What about Emily?"

Not trusting a baby-sitter to care for his baby, Luke had brought his daughter. The little girl instinctively seemed to know today was not a good day to fuss. All morning, she had played peaceably in her playpen or crawled around on all fours chasing after her daddy. Luke and Sydney had sidestepped her, given her wooden spoons to gnaw on and kept a watchful eye on her. But mostly, they'd tiptoed around each other.

"I thought I'd give her a bottle and put her in your room for a nap. We'll shut the door. No one will know she's here."

Doubts surfaced in her mind like corks bobbing in the water. Sydney picked at a glob of flour on her thumb. "Are you sure?"

"Positive. It's going to be great." He glanced at his watch. "Now, go."

Sydney patted her hair with her hand and glanced down at her flour-spotted jeans and T-shirt. She felt her smile waver as his gaze skimmed over her with an intense heat that caught fire inside her and spread clear down to her toes. "I could probably use a shower."

"Well, you look great to me." His voice sounded husky and inviting. "But your guests might expect you to have dressed up."

A blush heated her cheeks. "Right. It won't take me long."

Especially knowing she was naked in the shower with Luke in the same house! The thought electrified her nerve endings. She wondered if he had the same thought, and her blush deepened.

"I'll be right back."

"Take your time."

The doorbell chose that moment to ring. The sound echoed in Sydney's head. Panic froze her heart in the middle of a beat. She stopped, unable to move forward or backward.

"Oh, no!"

Luke smiled casually and walked past her. He paused for one brief, too-short second, to place his hands on her stiff shoulders. His touch was warm and stirred raw emotions deep inside her. "Relax." His silky voice did anything but calm her. "I'll get the door."

"Could it be a guest already?" she asked, panic making it difficult to draw a breath. Or was that Luke's effect on her? Confused, she looked to him for assurance.

Chuckling to himself, he twisted the brass knob. "Hello."

As he stuck out his hand in greeting, Sydney edged forward, fearful who it could be. Could it be her boss? Roxie? What if the V.P. of Management had arrived early and seen Sydney dressed like this...with a man opening *her* door like he lived here?

"I'm Luke," he said, stepping back to allow the person entrance to her house.

"I'm Jennie." That familiar energetic voice gave Sydney's heart a jolt. "You're as gorgeous as your sexy voice was on the phone."

His face reddening, Luke tipped his head to the side. "Sydney didn't tell me she had such a cute little sister."

"Cute!" Jennie brushed past him, her nose lifted toward the ceiling in outrage. "I guess that means you've already fallen for my sister, then." She offered both of them a friendly anything-going-on-here-that-I-should-know-about? grin. "That's the story of my life."

"W-what are you talking about?" Sydney managed, feeling Luke's gaze focus on her. His smile broadened, creasing his cheek with a dimple, and made her pulse thrum. "What are you doing here?"

"You know I loved Stan." Jennie rolled her blue eyes as she set her purse on the nearest chair.

"Is that why you tried to sabotage my wedding?"

Jennie harrumphed. "If I had, then I would have saved you a lot of grief." She hugged Sydney. "Hi, sis. Need some help?"

"W-what?" She felt her world spinning, and she looked to Luke for the answers that would stop this merry-go-round.

"You didn't tell her?" Jennie asked.

He shrugged. "Haven't had much time for anything but baking." He wiped his hands on the dish towel. "I thought you'd make a nice surprise."

"What's going on?" Sydney asked, placing a friendly arm around her little sister, who wasn't so little now that Jennie had grown two inches taller than her.

She hooked an arm around Sydney's waist. "Luke called and recruited the troops. Said you needed some help with a shower or something. So I rounded up the boys."

"Paul and Scott?" The fullness of Sydney's heart compressed her lungs, and she couldn't breathe. "They're coming too?"

"Yep, they should be here any minute. They were following me over, but I think I lost them."

She felt her brows knitting together. "Were you driving too fast?"

"They got stuck at a light. Don't worry so much, Mother Hen."

Sydney frowned with worry. She couldn't help it. She'd played the role of mother too often, fretted over her little chickadees too much to quit now.

"Jennie can help you with serving, and the guys can park cars or wash dishes. Whatever is necessary."

Sydney crossed her arms over her chest. "They're not touching our mother's crystal."

Jennie rolled her eyes again. "They're not eight years old anymore, Syd. They'll be careful." She gave her big sister a comforting squeeze. "Relax, will ya?"

Why did she suddenly feel they were standing on the edge of disaster? She loved her brothers and sister. She did. And she was moved by Luke's sweet gesture of tracking them down, but it only seemed as if more actors were falling into her nightmare.

Wondering how he'd managed to get hold of her busy sister when she couldn't ever get in touch with her, Sydney asked, "How did you track down Jennie?"

"Roxie. She found the number at your desk. I made the call."

"He has the dreamiest voice on the phone...in person, too." Jennie gave him a wink and a smile. "When are the guests arriving?"

"Soon," Luke answered.

"Then don't you think you should go get ready, sis? I mean, you don't want to look like a ragamuffin."

Sydney glanced one last time at the soufflé waiting to go in the oven and the small servings of crème brûlée waiting on the counter. What did she have to lose? Her heart almost burst with the knowledge that her siblings had cared enough to bail her out of a difficult situation. And she only had Luke to thank.

"How will I ever thank you for this?" Sydney asked as she backed through the kitchen door carrying the empty silver tray.

"Here." Luke took it from her. Their hands brushed. A hot flame shot through him. He wiped his brow with the sleeve of his shirt. He could think of a number of ways he'd be glad for her to thank him, starting with a breath-stealing kiss. He wasn't sure if she was still angry with him, or if she was simply nervous, jittery and standoffish today because of the party. But he didn't think it wise to mention that at the moment.

He wished he could grab her, kiss her and share his feelings, his longings. But did he dare? Not during the party. But afterward, he'd...he'd tell her. Before she got away.

"Need more baklava?"

She nodded. "And the chocolate mousse. The guests are eating it up like they've been on a fast for a week."

"How many more dishes do we have to wash?" Scott asked, his hands submerged in sudsy water.

"Yeah, can't we chauffeur cars or something?" Paul dried a delicate china teacup and placed it carefully on the counter.

"Not now," Sydney answered. Luke could see the family resemblance in Sydney's brothers and sister with their sky-blue eyes and autumn-red hair.

"I'll refill the tray, if you'll take the mousse into the dining room," Luke injected.

"Thanks." She met his gaze. Her warm blue eyes filled him with hope.

"What do we get for thanks?" Scott asked, reaching for another plate.

"Dishpan hands," Paul said.

"Exactly." Scott scowled, his freckled face matching his brother's.

Sydney shook her head at her two brothers, but her focus remained on Luke. "I'm sorry I was mad the other day when I found out—"

"It's okay, Sydney." He lined the tray with pristine doilies that looked feminine and charming. "I understand. I should have been the one to tell you."

"That's not the point. You'd already done so much for me. We'd already accomplished so much. I shouldn't have had any doubts at that point. I should have known you wouldn't let me down. And you didn't." She dipped her chin, as if searching for the answer. "I don't know why I doubted you...your abilities...the success of the party."

"I do."

She tilted her head and looked at him.

"Because I know you." And he did. But he wanted more. He didn't want to ever stop discovering her many facets. "You're not the type to depend on anybody. You handle everything. So, the fact that you needed help from someone else unnerved you."

She gave him a dazzling smile that made his stomach tangle in excited knots. "You're right. But it worked out perfectly." She placed a hand on his arm that sent flickers of heat through his body. "And you know what? Everybody seems to be having a wonderful time! Everyone has been raving over the food."

"Good."

"Maybe we've expanded your repertoire. You'll have to add some of these to your dessert list at the restaurant."

"It sold."

"It did?"

He nodded without regrets. "Thanks to you, I'm ready to start work on the website. You've expanded my horizons, Sydney."

Luke's heart hammered its way to his throat. She'd opened up doors of possibilities, shown him things he hadn't known about himself, proven he could care for his daughter, awakened him to the possibility of marriage.

"But I may need some more help."

"Anytime." Her voice dropped to a husky, intimate whisper and opened up whole new possibilities. His pulse quickened.

He prayed she'd keep her hand on his arm forever. It made him proud that she'd trusted him, relied on him. Thank God, he hadn't disappointed her. Relief made him want to wrap his arms around her and hold her tight. "Sydney—"

The kitchen door swung open and Jennie entered, her face flushed. "Do we have any more punch?"

Paul slapped a damp dish towel on the counter. "Throw some on Luke and Sydney."

"Yeah," Scott added. "It was getting steamy in here."

Jennie's eyebrows arched. She eyed Luke and her sister, a sly smile lurking at her lips that reminded Luke too much of Sydney. "Really now."

"Punch is in the fridge," he answered, stunned that he'd been only a heartbeat away from reaching for Sydney, from touching her, showing her how much he cared about her, how much he needed her.

Sydney cleared her throat. "I'll get the mousse."

"I'll stay here in the kitchen where I belong." And keep his hands to himself. But what about his heart? Had he already given it away?

She gave him a lopsided grin on her way to her guests and left him wondering if there was more to her gratefulness.

Jennie gave him a thumbs-up signal. "Going great."

He nodded, unable to speak, his throat clogged with a mixture of relief and bottled emotions that were bubbling to the surface. He knew at the end of the day Sydney would be ready to say goodbye to him and his daughter. But could he say it? He didn't think so.

"Can I get you anything, Roxie?" Sydney asked the mother-to-be.

"A waist like yours and those presents." Her brown eyes gleamed with excitement.

What Sydney would have given to be in Roxie's condition. She swallowed her own pettiness. "Give yourself a few months after the baby's born. But you don't have to wait that long for these presents.''

The guests gathered close, settling around the mother-to-be with anticipation as she began opening the wrapped gifts one by one. They passed the teddy bears and booties around so everyone could ooh and aah.

"A wonderful party, Sydney," Ellen Davenport said, biting into her fourth baklava. Her boss rolled her eyes heavenward as if she'd just entered paradise. "I don't think my mother made it this good. This is to die for."

"I'm glad you like it."

"Where did you find the recipe?"

"Oh, we sort of made it up as we went along."

"We?"

Heat singed her cheeks. "A friend helped." She knew he was more but she couldn't admit it to her boss. Not when she could barely admit it to herself. "He's an award-winning chef."

"Oh, how resourceful of you." Ellen gave her an approving nod, as if tabulating the points on her upcoming review.

"Sydney," Ann Baxter interrupted as she moved with her usual power play between them. The vice president gave her a hard stare. "I want to know where you got this crème brûlée."

"I-is there something wrong?" Her nerves tightened.

"I should say so. I've never had anything this scrumptious. I want to know where I can buy it."

Relief washed through her. She beamed and wished Luke could hear the compliments. "Well, you can't. I-I mean, we made it."

"You didn't buy it?"

"No, ma'am."

She laughed, the sound a staccato beat. "I would have had the whole thing catered."

Sydney's eyebrows arched. "But I thought you said...how special it would be if I made everything from scratch."

"Sure. And see how special the shower turned out. But I didn't expect this much. Who's got the time for this? I don't know how you did it all, what with work being a zoo these days."

"I confess I had a little help."

"From an award-winning chef," Ellen added.

"Really?" She spooned another serving into her mouth. "Who is it?"

Sydney nodded, feeling pride puff out her chest. "Luke Crandall."

Ann's brow wrinkled. "Never heard of him."

"He owned a restaurant in Dallas, but he sold it. Now, he's starting a website for single fathers."

"You'll have to give me the name of it," Ellen said, interest making her green eyes sparkle. "I've got several friends who are single dads. It's a tough job."

"Too bad he doesn't do catering," Ann grumbled.

Sydney made a mental note to mention it to Luke later. Later...she hoped he'd be around. Because she wasn't ready to see him go. Not yet. Not ever. Her heart tightened at the realization that she had nothing...no reason...to hang around him any longer. A clean break would be best.

"It's a good thing you hired some help, Sydney, for the party." Ellen wiped her fingers on the engraved napkin. "I'm impressed with how well you're handling everything."

"Good managerial skills," Ann noted. "You delegate authority well."

Sydney smiled. Words stuck in her throat. This is what she'd been hoping for. Then why did she feel like a horse up for auction?

"We've been watching you closely over the last few

weeks, Sydney," Ellen stated, her office face slipping into place.

"Someone's got to take Roxie's place. She won't be there much longer. Would you be interested?" Ann asked.

"Would I?" She couldn't think of any words except— yippee! Of course she wanted the promotion! What else did she want? Her stomach twisted into an uncertain knot. This was what she'd worked such long hours for. She'd put herself through the anguish of giving this baby shower. All for this moment! Instead of feeling exhilarated though, for some reason tears burned the backs of her eyes. She felt sick, her stomach pitching and turning.

"It'd be more responsibility," Ann added.

"But more pay." Ellen smiled.

She needed the money to help Jennie finish school. But the pride she'd thought she'd feel never materialized. Instead she felt boxed into a tight wedge.

"What's that noise?" Roxie paused in opening another gift. A startled hush fell over the guests, silencing the whispers and laughter throughout the room. Emily's cry sputtered then gained momentum.

Sydney's heart galvanized into a panicked cadence. What was wrong with Emily? Had something happened? She pushed one of Roxie's presents into Ann's hands.

"It's Luke's baby," she assured everyone. "I'll take care of her." With that brief explanation, she ran down the hall, her pulse racing with concern. Poor little Emily. She'd awakened in a strange place. She was probably frightened.

"Who's Luke?" someone asked behind her.

"A chef," Roxie said.

At the same time, Jennie answered in a loud, crystal-clear voice, "Sydney's boyfriend."

Sydney cringed. And at the same time felt her heart plummet, knowing he'd never be her boyfriend or anything more. He couldn't be.

Chapter Eleven

Cringing, Sydney entered her bedroom. The drapes had been drawn, and it took a second for her eyes to adjust. Baby Emily sat on her diapered behind in the middle of her playpen. Her baby-fine, dark hair stood in disarray, as if she'd tugged in frustration and fear at the locks. Tears streamed down her chubby, reddened cheeks.

"Oh, Emily. It's okay," Sydney cooed.

Before she picked up the baby, Luke arrived. "Is she okay?"

He lifted his daughter in his arms, cradling her, shushing her fears. Her little chubby arms looped around his neck. He jiggled her, walking around Sydney's bedroom with an up and down motion to his step.

Sydney reached out to smooth the baby's hair back into place, but she stopped herself. Her heart ached with the realization that Luke didn't need her, didn't look to her for help this time. And Emily didn't reach for her. She needed and wanted her daddy. In a choking voice, she managed to say, "I think she woke up and didn't know where she was. It scared her."

Emily snuffled against Luke's shirtfront. She gave a muffled sneeze, and he patted her back. With infinite care and gentleness, he wiped away his daughter's tears. The sweet gesture made Sydney long for him to be able to wipe away her fears, her heartache. But that was an impossibility.

"I guess I better get back to my guests," Sydney said, feeling like a fifth wheel.

"Wait," Luke said. His dark eyes studied her for a moment. "Would you mind holding her for a few minutes? I have the last batch of crème brûlée coming out of the oven any second."

"I can take care of that for you. Stay with your daughter."

He shook his head. "It's okay, Sydney." He shifted his daughter in his arms. "Wanna go visit the nice people and say hello?"

She gurgled her answer, and Luke smiled.

"See? She wants to go to the baby shower." He plunked his daughter into her arms and headed back to the kitchen by way of the back hallway, avoiding the living room full of women.

Sydney's heart felt as if it might burst with an emotion she hadn't experienced in years. She kissed the top of Emily's head. "You have a wonderful daddy, Emily. You're a lucky little girl."

"Da-da-da-da-da."

A moment later, with a gurgling Emily in her arms, she emerged from the bedroom and greeted her guests. What better attraction at a baby shower, she realized at that moment, than a real live baby!

"Oh! Isn't she adorable?"

"Look at those big brown eyes!"

"Cootchie cootchie coo!"

The women swarmed around Sydney, smiling at the baby, holding her little hands, tickling her under the chin.

Emily ate up the attention. She smiled and gurgled with delight. Suddenly, Sydney wondered if Roxie minded the intrusion on her special day.

"Maybe I should put her in the kitchen," she said in a low voice, as the women took their seats again around the mother-to-be and the coffee table full of gifts.

"No, please," Roxie said, tears swelling in her eyes. "She's the cutest little thing." She cupped her hand around the baby's fist. "Makes my pregnancy seem even more real."

Sydney felt her throat constricting. "Soon, you'll have your own baby." Her arms tightened around Emily's pudgy body. "Want to hold her?"

Roxie shook her head. "I don't think my lap is big enough." She ran a hand over her rounded stomach. "In fact, I think I lost my lap about three months ago. Besides, one baby kicking on the inside of my tummy is enough right now."

A few chuckles passed around the room. All eyes settled on the baby in Sydney's arms. The warm bundle made her heart feel light and happy. She tried to assure herself it was the fact she'd gotten the promotion, but she couldn't escape the truth.

"Sit here beside me—" Roxie patted the empty seat on the sofa "—so I can watch and play with her. She can help me open the rest of these presents."

Roxie finished opening her gifts, laughing at baby Emily who tried to grab the tiny infant outfits and plastic books. Sydney stayed busy prying paper and bows and soufflé out of the ten-month-old's hands. Hitching the little girl on her hip, she filled Roxie's cup with punch and scrounged up the last diamond of baklava for Ellen and one more serving of crème brûlée for Ann.

"You sure are coordinated," the V.P. commented, as

Sydney balanced Emily on one hip while wielding a plate of cheese and fruit in the other hand.

"All it takes is practice."

"And she had plenty," Jennie said, collecting empty plates and cups and carrying them into the kitchen.

"Oh?" Ellen's finely plucked eyebrows lifted.

Sydney shot her sister a warning look, but Jennie didn't seem to notice. "Yeah, she raised me, along with our brothers after our mother died."

The small group of women gave a collective "ah" of sympathy, understanding and respect.

"No wonder you're a natural," a woman Sydney didn't know said with a smile.

"And your sister and brothers came to help you out with the party!" someone else exclaimed. "You raised them right."

Roxie sighed and rubbed the edge of her rounded belly. "You should have children of your own, Sydney. You'd make a wonderful mother."

The words felt like a hard punch to her stomach. She felt her composure tremble. She managed a wobbly smile. "Thanks, but I've done my share."

"You're not thinking of getting married and deserting us like Roxie, are you?" Ann asked with a shrewd look on her face.

A picture of Luke filled Sydney's mind and heart. Her heart squeezed tight. Her mind shut out the possibility. Emily squirmed in her arms, and she realized she'd tightened her hold on the baby. "Uh, definitely not."

"That's good," Ann said. "Some women, like me, are made for careers, not family. You strike me as that type, Sydney. We're not cut out for cooking and cleaning and changing diapers."

Her words sliced Sydney deeply. She'd realized over the past few weeks that she liked cooking...that is, cooking with Luke. Her insides simmered at the thought. She didn't mind cleaning. In fact, scrubbing the kitchen floor somehow relaxed her, often took her mind off her troubles. And changing diapers...well, that had never bothered her. When she'd been a child taking care of her baby sister, it had been like playing house. Now, she almost wished Luke would ask her to change Emily's diaper once in a while.

She knew why he hadn't. Because of her bold statements of not wanting kids, of only wanting a career. If that's what she wanted, then why did she feel so empty inside?

"That's a shame," Roxie said, folding up some pink-and-blue wrapping paper. "I can't think of anything more fulfilling than having a baby, a family and a wonderful husband."

Sydney thought she'd melt right then and there into a bucket of tears. She swallowed back the emotions that poured out of her heart. She knew in that moment that Roxie was right. Nothing had ever fulfilled her like caring for Jennie, Paul and Scott. Nothing would ever fulfill her that way again, not her job, not a promotion, definitely not her lonely life. She felt the walls of her bleak existence fold in on her.

She wanted more than a stupid promotion. She wanted to feel needed again. She wanted to feel loved and cherished. She wanted a husband...somebody as wonderful and caring as Luke. But that was an impossibility. She wanted a baby...a sweet, bright-eyed baby like Emily. But that dream wouldn't come true.

Luke wouldn't want her if he ever learned the truth. But he wouldn't learn about her deficiencies if she could help it. He wanted more kids. He deserved them. He didn't deserve half a woman. And she was beginning to feel as if she'd missed out on some of the essential female genes.

Luke and Emily were a family now. They didn't need her anymore.

She gave a tremulous smile and felt her heart rip to shreds. "We all have to do what we're capable of doing."

"I thought they'd all never leave." Scott plopped down on the sofa and stuck his feet on the coffee table. "I'm exhausted."

Luke lifted Emily into his arms. "I think we can call this a definite success."

Having watched Sydney's brothers and sister work together, he realized he wanted a strong family unit for his daughter...for himself. But could he juggle everything as efficiently as Sydney seemed capable of doing?

He turned to smile at Sydney, but saw her duck her head and stumble into the kitchen.

"What did I do now?" Paul asked, stuffing another scoop of mousse into his mouth. "Scott, what'd you say?" He kicked at his brother's foot resting on the coffee table.

"Nothin'!"

Luke shook his head. "She's probably just tired."

"I'll go check on her," Jennie said.

"Let me." Luke handed Emily to Sydney's little sister.

"You are a cute little thing," she said, jiggling the little girl.

Luke followed Sydney into the kitchen. The door swung shut behind him. Sydney stood in front of the stove, her back to him. Her shoulders shook slightly and he heard her sniff. Concern etched a deep groove into his heart.

He put a hand on her back, felt her stiffen in response. "Are you okay?"

"Fine."

"The party was a success."

"Yeah, sure."

"Roxie said you got that promotion. The V.P. asked you to take her place when she leaves to have the baby."

"Yippee." Her voice cracked.

Slowly, he turned her toward him. His thumb moved with tenderness over her damp cheeks. He felt her tears burn their way into his heart. "What is it?"

"Nothing." She sniffed and tried to step away but backed into the stove. "I'm fine."

"Yeah, I can see that. Post-party blues? Is that it?"

"Yeah, I'm just so sorry it's over." She shook her head. "I bet you are, too. How come you aren't jumping up and down? Now, you don't have to put up with me anymore."

He shoved his hands into his back jeans pockets. "You want this to be goodbye?"

"You don't need me. And I don't have a cake to bake anymore."

"I thought we'd developed a friendship. We've shared a lot over the last few weeks. You've helped me with Emily. I think I helped you with this party. Truth is—" he swallowed the hard lump in his throat "—I don't want it to end."

Her eyes widened. "What?"

"I don't want to stop seeing you. The hell of it is I want to see more of you. I want—"

"No." She pushed away from him. "Stop. Don't say any more."

"Why?" He reached for her, but she sidestepped him.

"Because there isn't a future for us, Luke. There isn't—"

Confusion clouded his thinking, but his feelings burned brighter. "You must have been contemplating it yourself, or you wouldn't feel so adamant."

When she didn't respond, he prodded her with another question. "How do you know?"

"Because you have your own life. Your daughter. And I have mine."

"We're not going to rehash that career-oriented stuff, are we?"

"I have a new job."

Anger grabbed hold of his heart. Resentment tightened its grip on him. "I heard. So, because I have a baby, you wouldn't consider getting involved with me, is that what you're saying?"

Her mouth opened, but she said nothing.

Hot, fierce blood pumped through his veins. "Lie to yourself, Sydney, but I don't think that's your problem."

"You don't know anything about me, Luke."

"I know plenty. And what I know, I love." He paused, noticed her sharp intake of breath, felt the constriction around his chest ease. "Yeah, you heard me right." His confidence grew, fueled by his frustrations. "But the thing I don't like about you is when you pretend to be courageous and brave, forging your own life, when in reality you're a coward."

Her spine straightened like a dried piece of pasta. "I am not."

"Sure, you are. You're afraid, Sydney. Afraid you've chosen the wrong path. Afraid you'll be hurt like you were during your first marriage. Afraid you care for me as much as I care for you. Afraid you just might fall in love with Emily, too."

"Luke, you don't know what you're saying."

"Yes, I do. I've given it a lot of thought. In fact, that's all I've thought about for the last week. I need you, Sydney. Emily needs you."

Her head jerked, as if she might bolt and run.

Damn. He'd said the wrong thing. He'd scared her. He'd spoken like he wanted her for a nanny. "I don't want to hand my baby over to you. I want you to be my partner. You know what I realized this past week? That I don't enjoy cooking."

She faced him then, turning to look at him, shock widening her eyes. "What?"

"Without you. I don't enjoy anything without you being there. I want you to share my life with me."

Her face paled. "Luke—"

"I know this is sudden. But I've learned a lot over the last few weeks because of you. You showed me I'm not like my father. You showed me I can settle down. I can be responsible. I can have a family. I'm not afraid anymore, Sydney. Don't you be either. Take that giant leap. Believe with me. I'll catch you. I promise."

"Luke." Tears choked her voice. "I can't. You don't understand."

"Is it that you want your own baby? We can work on that. I know you've said you've raised all the kids you wanted, others' kids, not your own. But Emily would be your own. You'd see. And we'll have more." He reached for her then. "Sydney, let me love you. Let me into your heart."

She stood completely still. But when he wrapped his arms around her, drew her to him for a kiss, he felt a tremor rip through her. It rocked his senses. Dipping his head, cupping her chin, he kissed her, revealing to her all the emotions he'd been hiding, his longings and desires. He wanted this woman more than he'd ever wanted anything or anyone.

The kiss was a mixture of sweet longings and urgent passions. She opened to him, gave herself to him. He knew as she melted beneath him that her heart belonged to him, as much as his belonged to her. He had to help her realize it.

Then he tasted the saltiness of her tears. His heart contracted. He pulled back, smoothed his hand along her damp cheek. "What is it, Sydney?"

"Luke, I can't..." She pushed away from him. Wrapping her arms around her waist, she turned away from him. In a barely audible voice, she said, "I can't have any children. That's why my marriage fell apart. That's why Stan found another woman, a fertile one. So, this pretty little dream of yours is pure fantasy. It can't happen. Please, don't love me.''

Sydney ran out of her house, her purse hanging from her arm, her keys jangling. With numb fingers, she wrestled with the keys until she found the right one. She let herself into the haven of her car. The silence pulsed around her, punctuated by her heavy, labored breathing. For a moment, she sat there, drawing in gulps of inadequate air, and felt the tears pour out of her.

Her heart was breaking into pieces, like a glass figurine smashing to the floor. She leaned her head against the steering wheel and let the burning tears flow. Would there ever be enough tears to shed to rid her of her grief? Would she ever recover from her losses in life? First, not able to have a baby. And now, Luke.

She was a coward, just as he'd said. She'd been petrified to see the pity in his eyes when she told him the truth.

When Luke came to stand on her porch, she forced the key in the ignition and jerked the car into gear. She had to get away. She couldn't discuss this anymore. She didn't want his pity, his anger, his contempt. She knew at that moment, the only thing she wanted in this world was his love.

She'd had it, for a brief second. It had tasted like spring, full of possibilities, full of hope. She'd clung to him, wanting him, needing him, loving him, but knowing that their love could never blossom.

She drove for a long time, without a destination. She let her mind go numb, concentrated on the sound of the tires spinning over asphalt. But her heart ached, like it had never ached before. She'd hurt when she'd learned of Stan's betrayal. She'd hurt at the knowledge of her failed marriage. But honestly, she'd been more humiliated than hurt.

With Luke, she felt an aching emptiness that could never be filled. If only they'd met so many years before, before she'd known the truth. Then maybe they would have survived together. She couldn't see him rejecting her as Stan had. But if they'd met so long ago, then he wouldn't have Emily. And his daughter would sustain him now, no matter how much he hurt at her rejection of his love. The sad truth was that she had nobody.

Oh, for a brief moment, she'd had her family around her again, her brothers and sister. Thanks to Luke. It had been the sweetest gift she'd ever received. She knew now, it had come from his heart. It made hers throb even more.

Suddenly, she became more aware of her surroundings, the shade trees arcing over the narrow street. She pulled to the curb outside Luke's house. What had brought her here? Foolishness? Or a need to grieve over what might have been?

She leaned her head against the steering wheel and wept. Maybe God had decided she wasn't cut out for motherhood. Maybe she'd failed in some way while trying to raise her brothers and sister. Maybe Ann was right. Maybe some women weren't meant to have babies or husbands or families.

Through the fog filling her mind with doubts and self-incriminations, she heard a car door shut. Not until a gentle tapping on the window startled her did she realize she'd been followed by Luke. She stared at his ravaged face through the car window. He tried to open the door, but it remained locked. He motioned for her to get out of the car.

Gathering the tattered shreds of her composure, she blew her nose, wiped away her tears and pushed open the car door. She'd pretend she was fine. She'd pretend his words hadn't upset her. She'd go on pretending, because that was all she had left.

As she stepped from the car, he pulled her into his arms, buried his face against her neck and whispered in a hoarse, ragged voice, "I love you."

He held her so tight, she thought her circulation had been cut off. She felt woozy in his arms and at the same time like she'd found home. How could something so wonderful hurt her so much?

Trying to resist his allure, the tempting tone of his declaration, she wished for one minute she could give in to the fantasy, believe in it, in Luke. But she couldn't. Because in the end, it would all vanish. Her voice muffled against his chest, she whispered, "Where's Emily?"

"With Jennie." He smoothed his hands down her back, then hugged her tight again. "Oh, Sydney. I'm so sorry."

Her insides trembled in response. Biting down on her lip, she tried to stay sedate, but her heart bruised her breastbone.

"Can you forgive me?" He kissed her neck, her cheek, her lips. "I didn't know. I wouldn't have suggested..."

She placed a hand on his warm cheek. "I know. I couldn't tell you before. I couldn't handle your rejecting me."

"Rejecting you? I wouldn't... I love you, Sydney."

His words pierced her shell and crumbled her resolve. She dropped her face into her hands. Her shoulders began to shake. Once again, her world fell apart. This time, Luke couldn't put it back together.

He felt as helpless as when Emily cried. What could he do? Only one thing came to mind. He wrapped his arms around her, pulled her to his chest and let her cry, absorbing the shudders rocking through her. He felt her tears dampen his shirt.

As her weeping started to subside, he moved her toward

the porch, then inside his house. "This is where you belong."

"Luke, this can't happen. There can't—"

He smothered her protest with a kiss that rocked through his soul. "I love you."

"Luke—"

He kissed her again, kissed her hard, until he blocked out her protests from his mind, until he felt her body soften against him. He knew she wasn't rejecting him. She'd rejected herself.

"Luke—"

He dipped his head to kiss her again, but she covered his mouth with her fingertips. "Listen to me." Her voice sounded stronger than he felt. "You can't understand what I'm going through. I *can't* have a baby. Ever. I've seen every doctor imaginable. It's impossible. This is impossible."

She leaned into him, this time her arms wrapping around his torso, as if she never wanted to let him go. He brushed a kiss across her temple. This time, he let her speak, let her pour out her heart to him.

"You can't understand what it feels like. You have Emily."

"That's garbage." His harsh tone made her flinch.

"Don't you understand? You're not alone in this. But you push others away. You're pushing me away. When you could have it all."

She pulled away from him, her tear-ravaged face growing red with equal anger. "Damn you. You have your little piece of immortality. But there will never be a piece of me left here on earth when I'm gone." She took a ragged breath. "Even though my mother didn't live long, she left four children who resemble her, just as Emily looks like you. What will I leave behind? Nothing. For some reason,

God didn't think I'd make a good mother. But please, for God's sake, don't pity me."

"Pity you?" He balled his hands into fists. "I could throttle you."

"What?"

"I'm angry at you. I'm mad as hell that you can't have children, for whoever or whatever is responsible. And I could shoot Stan for making you feel like a second-class citizen.

"Don't you realize what you've done? Can't you see the effect you've had on your siblings? You've put so much of yourself, the most important part—your heart and soul—into raising your brothers and sister. Because you sacrificed for them, because you loved them as their mother couldn't, they've grown up into loving, caring adults." He lifted her tear-stained face to meet his gaze. "Don't you understand? *They* are your legacy. They are your piece of immortality.

"And you're the woman that completes me. Not because you're good with kids or with Emily. But because you're good with life. I need you to be a part of me, a part of my life."

He looked deeply into her waterlogged eyes. "Tell me the truth. Does Emily cause you pain? Does she make you long for what you can't have?"

She shook her head. "At first...maybe. But now she makes me long to be a part of her life...your lives. I love Emily. As if she were my own."

He kissed her soundly, stealing her breath away. "I love you, Sydney Reede. And I want you to be my wife."

"Luke—"

"I've never asked a woman to marry me before. I don't ask you lightly. I want to wake up with you every day, and hold you as I fall asleep each night. I don't want to live without you.

"Honestly, I can't think of any greater gift to give my

daughter than a mother with your compassion and strength. Whether we have any more kids isn't a concern. Maybe we can adopt more. But we can decide that later. Frankly, I never thought I'd have a child at all. You've helped show me I'm not like my dad. I'm my own man. As you're your own woman.

"Marriage isn't a roll of the dice. It's a lifetime promise to love, not to be broken but to be shared—the good and the bad. I love your good and bad qualities, Sydney Reede. I love your smile, your warmth, your compassion and logic and perfectionism. You have a bright, keen mind. You challenge me, like no one ever has. But you also drive me a little crazy. You're always punctual. You're not very spontaneous. But you're getting better." He gave her a smile she couldn't resist.

"I think you're wearing off on me."

"Good. Together, in our own unique way, we'll be a family."

"Oh, Luke—"

He kissed her again, afraid of what her response would be. What if she pushed him away again? How would he survive? As he kissed her, he tried to think of another argument to get her to stay with him, to love him, to marry him. But her warm lips against his made his brain fuzzy.

"Luke." She broke away from him. She placed her hands against his chest. "Let me finish this time. Okay?"

He nodded, his heart beating in his throat.

Her eyes filled with fresh tears. "I love you, too. And I love Emily. For whatever reason that you love me, I'm grateful. This doesn't seem real. But if you think we can make a family, then I want to be a part of it."

Wrapping her arms around his neck, she kissed him, before he could draw a breath or say another word.

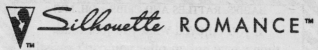

If you enjoyed what you just read,
then we've got an offer you can't resist!

Take 2 bestselling
love stories FREE!
Plus get a FREE surprise gift!

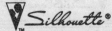

*This August 1999, the legend
continues in Jacobsville*

DIANA PALMER

LOVE WITH A
LONG, TALL TEXAN

A trio of brand-new short stories featuring
three irresistible Long, Tall Texans

GUY FENTON, LUKE CRAIG
and CHRISTOPHER DEVERELL...

This August 1999, Silhouette brings readers an
extra-special collection for Diana Palmer's legions
of fans. Diana spins three unforgettable stories of
love—Texas-style! Featuring the men you can't get
enough of from the wonderful town of Jacobsville,
this collection is a treasure for all fans!

*They grow 'em tall in the saddle in Jacobsville—and
they're the best-looking, sweetest-talking men to be
found in the entire Lone Star state. They are proud,
hardworking men of steel and it will take
the perfect woman to melt their hearts!*

**Don't miss this collection of original
Long, Tall Texans stories...available in
August 1999 at your favorite retail outlet.**

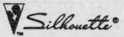

Silhouette®

THE MACGREGORS OF OLD...

#1 *New York Times* bestselling author

NORA ROBERTS

has won readers' hearts with her enormously popular MacGregor family saga. Now read about the MacGregors' proud and passionate Scottish forebears in this romantic, tempestuous tale set against the bloody background of the historic battle of Culloden.

Coming in July 1999

REBELLION

One look at the ravishing red-haired beauty and Brigham Langston was captivated. But though Serena MacGregor had the face of an angel, she was a wildcat who spurned his advances with a rapier-sharp tongue. To hot-tempered Serena, Brigham was just another Englishman to be despised. But in the arms of the dashing and dangerous English lord, the proud Scottish beauty felt her hatred melting with the heat of their passion.

Available at your favorite retail outlet.

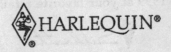

HARLEQUIN®